GUIDEPOSTS

GUIDEPOSTS

CHURCH CHOIR MYSTERIES™

The Blue Plate Perils

Roberta Updegraff

Guideposts®

CARMEL, NEW YORK 10512

www.guidepostsbooks.com

www.guidepostsbooks.com
Series Editor: Michele Slung
Cover art by Robert Tanenbaum
Cover design by Wendy Bass
Interior design by José R. Fonfrias
Interior cat illustrations by Viqui Maggio
Typeset by Composition Technologies, Inc.
Printed in the United States of America

With all my love to my children:
Mark Claire, Sarah and Kathryn.
We share memories, history and the future.
But, most importantly, we share love—family.

Acknowledgments

IT IS WITH GREAT ADMIRATION that I dedicate this book to the World War II partisan heroes in Luca Pedeferri's family: both those who are still alive, and also those who gave their lives for freedom in opposition to Mussolini's Fascists.

Thank you, also, to the American troops who fought alongside these partisans.

You gave us the freedom we enjoy, and ensured the democracy that we treasure. It seems that in each family, in every generation, are kindred spirits who recognize the value of story and history. I could not have created the character of Maddie without the help of my dear Italian friend, Luca. His respect for his family, and their contribution to the cause of Italian liberation, touched me greatly. We both cherish family history, the legacy that shapes us as individuals and as human beings. This legacy should never be forgotten.

The
Blue Plate
Perils

GRACIE STOPPED IN THE MIDDLE of her living room and drew a deep happy breath of familiarity. Her visit to Arlen, her son, and his family in New York had been wonderful, but she had missed her old house, and Willow Bend, in particular. This little Indiana town had been her home for more than half her life, and its people her chosen family.

She closed her eyes, listening to Marge Lawrence bustle about, making sure that Gracie's return and resettlement was not a one-woman task. Marge was not only her next door neighbor, she was also Gracie's closest friend.

They *were* different. Gracie was always one to wade into the water, whereas Marge would plunge right ahead, meeting challenges like a surfer greeting a wave. The most impulsive thing Gracie had done in years was dye her hair red. When she'd bemoaned her strawberry curls losing their youthful luster, and her secret longing for fiery hair again, Marge had bought a coloring kit and wrapped it in birthday paper. It didn't matter to her friend that Gracie's actual birthday wasn't for months.

Gracie loved red—red anything. Red declared *yes* to life! And she needed that reminder after El died. Her husband of more than thirty years had been her lover and best friend, so she had few memories that weren't wrapped in his love. And El had died so tragically—a freak accident on a local road.

Gracie ran her fingers through her curly mop, realizing that the decision that day really had made all the difference. She had not only restored her hair color, but also her attitude. Memories no longer ambushed her, sending her into a tailspin. From that day on, come as they would, Gracie allowed them to wash over her, treasuring their bitter sweetness. They became confirmation of a life well lived. El was still with her.

But, oh Lord, there still isn't a day goes by that I don't miss that man.

Behind her, Rocky Gravino crossed the threshold loaded with luggage, grumbling to Uncle Miltie. Rocky had insisted on carrying her bags, even though she'd attempted to hoist them out of the trunk herself. He had nudged her aside, chivalrously balancing them in each hand and under his arms.

She could only acquiesce, secretly hoping that his stubbornness wouldn't put his back out. Rocky suffered frequent discomfort, blaming his mattress for what Gracie suspected was simply aging. Rocky *was* seven years her senior, but Gracie was definitely a young sixty-two.

The editor of the local newspaper, Rocky sometimes intimidated folks with his brusqueness and unrelenting pursuit of truth. But she'd experienced his tender side, too. This man also knew the phantom ache of living without one's "better half." Rocky was a widower himself, though childless. He had a soft spot for stray animals and kids who were hurting.

Uncle Miltie ambled in behind Rocky. It was a good day for his osteoarthritis, and his cane not only supported his weight but gave him an advantage over his friend. At that moment, he was using it to point Rocky in the direction of the stairs, goading him on by declaring that "carrying bags builds muscle."

"Heard a good joke today," Uncle Miltie called out. When they gave him their attention, he grinned, "Don't tell me if you've already heard it, because I want to hear myself tell it again!" This tendency of his—tolerated, usually with groans—to delight in his own corny humor had earned him his nickname. "Uncle Miltie" was the name of a once-famous comedian, while Gracie's uncle had been christened George Morgan.

"One night, a man dreamed he was a teepee. The next night he had the same dream, except he was a wigwam. He keeps having the same dreams over and over, so he goes to his therapist. Tells the doctor about his dreams, and asks what they mean."

Uncle Miltie paused, waiting for someone to ask for the punch line. Gracie humored him. "So what did the doctor tell him?"

"'You're just *too tense!*'" Get it?" Gracie couldn't help but laugh. It was perhaps the surest sign she was home again.

Uncle Miltie thumped his cane on the floor a couple of times for effect, before pressing Rocky to take the luggage to Gracie's bedroom—upstairs, second door on the left.

"Mama's home!" Marge declared, carrying an indignant Gooseberry.

Gracie turned just in time to see her plump pumpkin tabby bound to the floor and head right for her legs, where he started rubbing and purring until he was picked up. "Hey, big boy!"

Gooseberry nuzzled her neck and cheek, his raspy motor of a purr filling her with delight. "I missed you!"

"I think the feeling is mutual." Marge grinned.

Her own little Shih Tzu, Charlotte, barked, and Marge bent to pick her up. "I don't think Uncle Miltie gave Gooseberry enough attention," Marge said, rubbing the dog's head. "But then, we're probably talking 'bottomless pit' here, even I have to admit."

She then headed for the kitchen to fix refreshments. Rocky had come back downstairs, and was leaning against the banister with his arms crossed. His expression confirmed that he, too, was happy to have her back.

A bit embarrassed by her rush of affection for her old friend, Gracie reached for the stack of mail, as her uncle explained that he had sorted it by level of importance. She gave him a quick peck on the cheek.

"By the way," Uncle Miltie called over his shoulder. "I fixed those broken slats on the rose trellis."

He dismissed her thanks with a wave of his hand. "A man's got to earn his keep."

"You miss me, too?" Rocky asked when Uncle Miltie disappeared into the kitchen.

Gracie kept her focus on the junk mail. She was not willing to admit how much she really had missed him. She and Marge had spoken on the phone, but Gracie had not talked to this, her second-best friend, since she'd left a month earlier for her son's apartment in New York.

El and Rocky had bonded as friends almost from the first day the newspaper editor had arrived from Philadelphia. The two men spent so much time together, it seemed natural Rocky would become her protector and confidant after El had died. That role had matured into a friendship Gracie valued greatly.

Marge liked to tease Gracie that Rocky was smitten with her. At this moment, standing in companionable silence, Gracie suspected there could be more if she would encourage him . . . but she couldn't do that. They were much too close for romance.

"So what's the news in Willow Bend?" Gracie asked.

He nodded toward the kitchen. "Smells like coffee."

"You're right!" Gracie had caught a whiff, too.

Rocky headed for the kitchen, Gracie following.

"Think Marge has provided some dunkers?" Gracie asked. How a person could drink crumb-saturated fluid, Gracie couldn't imagine, but Rocky considered coffee naked without a cookie.

He replied happily. "On the way to the airport, she told me she'd baked. And knowing your catering assistant's culinary skills, they're hard as rocks!" Another grin. "Perfect for dunking."

Marge was less enamored of cooking and baking than Gracie, but she'd embraced her chum's venture into catering with zeal. Gracie was willing to trust the cookies on the plate in front of her; after all, Marge was probably using one of *her* recipes.

"So *nothing* is new in Willow Bend?" Gracie prompted again. Her attention was drawn to the open cupboard door where she kept canned and dry goods, but she resisted the urge to do inventory. There would be time to make a grocery list when everyone left.

"Mmm-hmm!" Gracie said, tasting a peanut-butter cookie and looking around expectantly.

Rocky swallowed his soggy cookie, took another gulp and began to answer. "You might be interested to hear that there's a fellow snooping around Willow Bend."

"Gordon Welty isn't snooping," Marge corrected. "Sophie, Abe's sister, somehow started the ball rolling and pointed him in this direction."

Rocky acknowledged her explanation with a slight scowl. "Anyway, the man is looking to buy some property. Says he wants to start a new restaurant. He's a businessman."

"He's looking at the Carruthers place," Marge told her. "You know, that worn-down Victorian right behind Abe's Deli. Of course, Welty needs to respect our restoration campaign, and keep the historical society involved, but I don't see any problem."

Gracie made a mental note that it was time she paid a visit to John and Maisie Carruthers—whose house she knew very well—at the retirement residence where they now lived. They, like their house, had weathered a long, difficult life. Almost ninety, John and Maisie had outlived most friends and siblings. Their children had moved to other states and seldom made time to visit. To Gracie, though, they would always be cherished friends.

Gracie could almost see Maisie sitting in Eternal Hope's second pew, her gloved hands folded on her lap. A lady always wore a hat, and so Maisie did, even after it had stopped being fashionable. John spent most afternoons fussing with his meticulously manicured rose bushes, and Gracie knew it had been heart wrenching to see the garden decline along with the house as it got more and more strenuous for them to keep up.

Uncle Miltie cleared his throat. "Welty isn't planning some swanky eatery. There's no certainty Willow Bend could support one, anyway. What he wants is to open a franchise fast-food establishment. I doubt whether he's thinking of remodeling. Besides, I thought he was looking at Abe's place."

Rocky looked over his coffee cup. "Abe doesn't want to sell."

"I'm lost," Gracie said, trying to sort things out. "And, besides, Sophie doesn't live here."

Marge leaned back against the counter. "Remember, Gracie, I told you about it on the phone. It doesn't matter if Sophie's in Cleveland. She still thinks it's time for her brother to retire. She wants Abe to help her buy a place in Florida. She knew some people who knew Gordon Welty. Next thing, he was on the spot, pitching Abe his plan."

"But Abe wouldn't hear of it," Rocky reminded her.

Marge eyed him. "That's why he's looking at other possibilities. He told me as much." And to Gracie. "Good-looking fellow. When he laughs, the lines around his eyes crinkle in the cutest fashion." She paused. "Why is it that on men they're called laugh lines, and on us they're crow's feet?"

"Big-city fellows make me nervous. They don't have a clue

about small-town folks." Uncle Miltie ignored Marge's question. "*Demographics* is the word that city slicker uses to describe us. He's looking to cash in on families who are in a hurry. That's how I see it."

Marge frowned. "You make him sound so terrible!"

"Wake up and smell the coffee, dear girl." Uncle Miltie took a sip of his.

"Smells to me like money. And how can that be bad for our community?" Marge smiled smugly.

Uncle Miltie picked up a cookie. "Can't beat homemade."

"You're talking in riddles." Marge crossed her arms. "I think Gordon Welty's restaurant sounds like a vote of confidence in Willow Bend's future. And if Abe *does* decide he wants to retire, it seems like a perfect arrangement. Besides, there's already a Chinese restaurant for take-out."

Uncle Miltie leaned back in his chair. "Home cooking is *home cooking*. It's more than a recipe or store-bought ingredients; it's family. And it's *not* chow mein, either. These days folks are in too big a hurry. Kids deserve a hot, home-cooked meal and dinner-table conversation every night. There ought to be a law on the books declaring as much."

"I don't see how one negates the other." Marge's tone seemed a bit edgy. Gracie sensed that while she'd been gone, they'd had this same argument.

Gracie eyed her relative, signaling him to drop the conversation. It was Marge who carried it on. "Seems to me faster food would improve things. Families can eat at their dining room tables, and enjoy even more time together."

"We don't need city troubles invading our town," Uncle Miltie insisted. "Those places end up as hangouts for kids."

Marge rolled her eyes. "So one little restaurant is going to destroy the Willow Bend nuclear family, and encourage local gangs to organize! Buy motorcycles, even!"

"Parents will plop a bag down on a TV tray instead of sitting down to a nice meal." He looked stubbornly at her.

Marge was not going to give up. "They can do that as well with anything from the frozen food department . . . or even *home*-cooked dishes."

Gracie held up her hands stop-fashion. "I'm not getting involved until I know more. So let's call a time-out."

However, she added, "Sharing meals *does* seem to draw people closer."

"My point exactly." Uncle Miltie looked at Marge. "I don't think Gordon Welty is good for our town. I sense it in my bones!"

Gracie was beginning to get an uncomfortable feeling about this subject.

"I'm inclined to agree with Gracie's wise old uncle on this one, Marge," Rocky said calmly. "But let's talk about something a bit less charged, for now, anyway. Gracie just got home."

"Times are changing," Marge said, not letting it drop.

"Today's families have two working parents and busy children. There's no question there's a growing appetite for fast food, plus it means no one has to labor over a hot stove, or wash tons of dishes."

Uncle Miltie was not going to let their neighbor have the final word. "Why does it have to be labor? Gracie and I clean up together. We've had some of our best discussions loading the dishwasher."

Gracie smiled in affirmation, even though her uncle usually begged off, using one of his many favorite television shows as an excuse.

Rocky winked at her over his coffee cup, acknowledging her diplomacy. "I guess I'll add another two cents to the pot," he said, re-entering the fray. "I can only guess at the effects of franchised food on family dynamics, and I certainly can't speak to the quality of time spent cleaning up after supper."

He made eye contact with each of them. "But I *do* know a little bit about Willow Bend *geographics*. Abe has the best location in town. I don't care what the man says about being interested in the Carruthers place, it's Abe's building he's got his mind on."

He looked at Marge. "Welty says he wants a prime central location, not an edge-of-town site, and so he'd be nuts to challenge Abe's established popularity by putting a restaurant so close by the Carruthers place. Think about it. Folks stop there all the time to pick up a quart of chicken soup or a cheesecake for dessert. Who's going to frequent somewhere new when we've got Abe Wasserman?"

Uncle Miltie took a gulp of coffee. "Exactly. He'd be starting us on a slippery slope to losing touch with our traditions. Of which Abe's Deli is one of the best."

"I'm all for progress," Rocky went on, "don't get me wrong. And you're right, Marge, these convenience-food places are springing up all over the country. But I'm not convinced, either, that they're great for Willow Bend."

Marge put her hands on her hips. "Abe closes at six, remember? A lot of people don't finish work until after that! And besides, Welty wants to sell things like mashed potatoes and rotisserie chicken—family fare. It's different from Abe's and from Imperial City, too."

"Just who *is* this Welty, anyway?" Gracie cut in. "You said Sophie made the connection to him, but who *is* he, really?"

Marge reached for the coffeepot and topped everyone's cups. "He spoke at her investment club—you know, one of those women-only groups we were toying with starting. Anyway, Welty owns a couple of family-style, eat-in or to-go restaurants in other small towns, and he's already thinking about franchising. He needs investors. He wants to launch a couple more to prove the idea's feasibility. He's done the research, at least—or so he tells me." Marge paused, and Gracie could almost read her thoughts.

Marge, she knew, was remembering her experience with

her third husband. He had run out on the marriage, taking advantage of her financially. But Marge had managed to turn that heartbreak and disappointment into a new life as a successful businesswoman. Owner now of a gift shop that sold everything from greeting cards to novel fashion accessories, Marge still had reason to be wary of men with more schemes than sense.

"Gordon thinks a place specializing in simple family fare with the emphasis on take-out is the up-and-coming market." She smiled at Rocky. "A few chains already exist and are doing *very* well."

Rocky held her gaze. "I still think he wants Abe's place. And he's going to buy the Carruthers house and tear it down for a parking lot."

Marge shrugged. "I guess he's considering all his options. Good business sense."

Uncle Miltie wagged a finger. "Good *business* sense doesn't guarantee good *common* sense—and I mean *common* as in '*common* good of the community.'"

"As I remember," Rocky continued, "they discussed parking lots at great length at the town meeting a few months back. We all seemed to agree about keeping them to a minimum."

"Well, Abe's not going to sell." Gracie was trying to be confident. Willow Bend's most popular restaurant owner was not ready to retire, regardless of what his sister thought.

Marge, Gracie now recalled, had told her on the phone

that Sophie had suggested that perhaps her brother was getting too old to manage his place. But Gracie knew well how Abe had always said his sister acted more like his mother than a sibling.

It seems Abe had left a pot of coffee to boil over overnight, apparently sending Sophie into a tizzy, when she'd heard of it. Gracie herself was guilty of similar episodes of forgetfulness. Why, she'd bought an iron with an automatic shut-off just to double-check herself. Such lapses weren't of themselves confirmations of senility.

Besides, Abe wasn't *that* much older than Gracie, and he was a whole lot younger than Uncle Miltie.

She looked at her uncle. He didn't miss a trick. He had a mind for measurements that awed Gracie. He could change centimeters to inches, talk in kilometers as easily as miles. That was a skill *she* had never mastered!

Although educated only in the "school of hard knocks," as he called it, Abe was a brilliant man. Gracie loved her exchanges with him; Abe Wasserman was a sage in every sense of the word, one who had often made her see matters more clearly after their conversations.

"Why is it that a lot of our contemporaries deem Florida synonymous with retirement?" She asked no one in particular. "They seem to think productivity ends with Social Security. Can't older people produce a second crop—a third or a fourth—and continue to bloom again, right where they're planted?"

As much as she respected Sophie, Gracie just couldn't believe Abe would be happy moving to Florida. It made her mad just thinking of Sophie putting pressure on her brother because *she* wanted to vegetate in the sunshine. Didn't the woman realize Abe Wasserman's place was practically a landmark for Indiana hospitality? And one Gracie wanted to see remain in Willow Bend for a long, long time!

D O YOU THINK ROCKY IS RIGHT?" Marge asked, bending to take the clean plates out of the dishwasher. "I really don't want to see John and Maisie's place bulldozed for a *park*ing lot. It is dilapidated, that's true, but it has charm. It could be a city treasure, if someone invested some TLC."

She hugged the clean plates. "Wouldn't Cordelia Fountain have a *fit* if she suspected as much? She's on a campaign to preserve all the historical places. She's the one who suggested we get old-fashioned 'gas' streetlights."

"They certainly *look* authentic," Gracie had to admit. "You would never guess they're electric. Yes, Cordelia's idea certainly helped launch the town's preservation plan."

Marge chuckled. "We could sic her on Welty if we discover he really is serious about tearing down that old place.

Cordelia would never stand for it. John and Maisie's house is one of her 'Grand Ladies.'"

Gracie smiled, remembering the woman's ferocity for preserving the past. Cordelia had pestered Rocky until he gave her tourist home a full-page spread in the *Mason County Gazette's* weekend edition. That feature helped give her even more clout in archival circles and cemented her leadership of the Willow Bend Historical District Preservation Committee. Cordelia was a force to be reckoned with, all right, but Gracie hoped things wouldn't come to that.

"There's really nothing to worry about," she told Marge, still trying to convince herself. "Abe is *not* going to sell. He's not ready to retire. He professes the same philosophy as Miltie—he would rather wear out than rust out.

"Besides, Abe loves this town almost as much as he loves that deli. He could never be happy in one of those retirement communities in Florida. One day, he'll just hang up his apron for a smock at the daycare center in the senior center. Like Uncle Miltie, he loves going there to read stories to the children, even if he rarely gets the chance."

"I hope you're right."

"Earlier today, you sounded so gung-ho about Welty's project. What changed your mind?"

Marge sighed. "Lord knows how I hate to admit it when the guys are right . . . but I helped sponsor the 'Vote No To Macadam' campaign, remember? I'm with Cordelia on preserving Willow Bend's special charm. I do *not* want us to go the route of other small towns. We may not have planned it, but Willow Bend has remained the epitome of midwestern Americana. Our Main Street is just that—the *main street.*"

Marge leaned against the counter again. "You can walk from one end of the town to other, talk to people, stop for a soda and never feel like you've strayed too far from home. In Willow Bend, home is not only the place you start from, but also the one you return to, probably until the day you die. A cozy circle, if you ask me."

"Paving over property to make parking lots does have a way of changing things," Gracie agreed, "foisting us into the fast lane, as Uncle Miltie would say. Perhaps against our will, but doing it all the same."

"Besides, I've drawn my line on asphalt," Marge said with conviction. "And you know me when I take a stand!

"I guess it never crossed my mind anyone would think seriously about destroying one of those houses," Marge continued. Her expression softened. "Willow Bend is picture-postcard pretty. I never seem to get tired of it."

"Uncle Miltie is fond of saying that Willow Bend is the closest place to paradise this side of the Pearly Gates."

"That it is," Marge agreed. And glancing toward the living room, she lowered her voice. "I know he won't admit it, but he was like a lost puppy without you. I think we watched a hundred *Murder She Wrote* reruns, with him reminding me as many times how you're the better sleuth. You would have solved every one of those cases!"

Gracie laughed.

Marge reached to hug her. "I missed you!"

"It was only a month."

"Thirty days too long."

"Did I tell you that the Cantrells have an exchange student?" Marge said, changing the subject. "A girl from Italy. I forget her name, but she's as cute as a button."

"Matilde." Uncle Miltie reappeared in the doorway. "Gravino forgot his planner. Left it laying on the telephone stand. I think I'll mosey over and see if I can catch up with him at the newspaper office."

"You want me to drive you?" Gracie asked.

He shook his head. "Nice day for taking my constitutional."

"How do you know the girl's name is Matilde?" Marge wanted to know.

"Had an Aunt Matilda—persnickety old gal. She always got *my* bedroom when she came to visit—for what felt like months." He smiled. "Then there was my sixth-grade teacher, Matilda Winters. Now *there* was a sourpuss! So you see, the girl's name hit me right off. *Matilde* is no kind of name for such a pretty little pixie." He leaned on his cane. "They call her Maddie, though, so that's a bit better." He chuckled. "*Muddy*, she pronounces it. I love Italian accents." A grin. "Hey, you know what a specimen is?"

"I'm sure it's *not* what I think." Gracie said.

"A specimen," he said with exaggerated emphasis on the syllables, "is an Italian astronaut."

Marge groaned.

"Seriously now, Maddie told me Matilde was her grandmother's name, and that that woman raised her. And her mother lives in Cleveland. I could tell there's pain surrounding those two facts, but I didn't pry."

Gracie realized, "You know a lot about her."

"Met her at Abe's place a few times. She helps with Amy's shift. Abe is tickled to get two employees for the price of one.

"Now, *there's* a cute kid, that Cantrell girl. Amy's always got time for us mature folks. So many of the teenagers won't give the oldsters the time of day. Not so with Amy! She's a peach, all right."

Amy was often shy with her own age group, but Gracie had noticed she seemed quite at ease with the senior crowd in their church choir, despite being the only young person in the group. The girl had a beautiful voice, too. Soprano. Herself an alto, Gracie always admired singers able to hit those high notes.

"Each Sunday while you were gone, Amy came up to me after church asking about you and Gooseberry," Uncle Miltie told her. "Maddie's been with her most of the time. She doesn't say much—still a bit shy of all of us, I guess." Another grin. "But I've been softening her up with my jokes and stories."

Gracie could just imagine!

"Surprised me, her being Italian," Marge said. "She's got blue eyes. I expected all Italians to have dark eyes! She has shiny ebony hair, though, with a beautiful natural wave. Shame she wears it pulled back so often in a severe ponytail. The one day she had it down, I noticed how much prettier she looked. I have a mind to suggest she let it down more often.

"She has a lovely *caffé latte* complexion," Marge went on, carefully choosing a phrase to express her description with precision. She was a whiz with a color wheel—her home and shop decor were evidence of that flair. Marge was the first person Gracie knew to trade Harvest Gold for Almond appliances. And salmon was not a shade Gracie would have chosen for a living room, but in Marge's, it was elegant.

"Maddie's from the north of Italy, you know," Uncle Miltie was saying. "France and Switzerland are just a stone's throw. I spent some time in the Alps after the war ended. Met a lot of brave Italians—partisans. The country was in a shambles, but the people had an indomitable spirit."

He paused, looked past her, perhaps remembering that time. "*Umm*, terrible times, but at the same time hopeful. I knew the Italians would make it—told Maddie as much. I think that was the real ice-breaker between us. We've been friends ever since."

This was a new "war story" for Gracie. Uncle Miltie loved

to recount the less painful of his World War II experiences, but he had never mentioned Italy before. She was curious, but not sure this was the time to get him started on that tangent. Her uncle did have a tendency to milk every telling for the maximum effect and narrative duration. "Sounds like the two of you have hit it off," she said instead.

"She shared a little bit of her family history. Her grandparents' house had a tunnel that was used by the Italian freedom fighters. I've been through the area. It was kind of special, us having that in common."

"Well, Sophie sure seems to have taken a shine to the girl," Marge said. "I was talking to her the other day, and the woman could not stop singing Maddie's praises. She said she had always wanted a daughter. They have an Italian connection, too."

"Maddie told me that *Signora* Sophie reminds her of her deceased grandmother," Uncle Miltie said.

"You're always teasing me about knowing everything that goes on in this town," Gracie pointed out. "But it seems *you* have the scoop this time. Is Sophie actually living with Abe right now while she tries to hustle him down to sunny Florida?"

"You've got it," he replied. "And she's threatening to sell her apartment back home."

It suddenly dawned on her that the price he'd paid to glean all this information may have been in cholesterol, if he'd gathered it with Rocky at Abe's Deli. Gracie narrowed her gaze. "Rocky told me he ate most of his meals at the deli while I was gone. I suppose you were with him."

Uncle Miltie feigned innocence.

"You develop a taste for Abe's breakfast special, too?" she wanted to know. Rocky loved Abe's egg-and-bagel sandwich with home fries. Truth be known, the man had a weakness for about everything that wasn't good for him.

She worried more about health issues these days. After all, none of her dear ones were getting any younger, and she couldn't bear the thought of losing any of them. Gracie sighed inwardly, wishing Rocky would take better care of himself.

"Okay, okay!" Uncle Miltie said, coming clean. "Gravino and I ate there quite often. But look at it this way: we're helping to keep the guy in business! His sister claims he's barely in the black. Rocky and I did our best to remedy that!"

Gracie was now even more worried about her friend, realizing Abe's Deli might have financial problems as well.

Opening the door of Abe's Deli, Gracie was wonderfully ambushed by the apple-and-cinnamon scented air. Rocky, already perched on his stool, beckoned her to join him.

She straddled the stool beside his. There was nothing like Abe Wasserman's apple strudel—except maybe his potato kugel, or his cheesecake. . . .

"It's good to have you home, Gracie!" Abe came around the counter wiping his hands on his apron. He gave her a big, kitchen-scented embrace.

Rocky smiled. "Yep, it sure is good to have Gracie back. A month is too long to go without her cooking. No offense to you, Abe, but I miss her supper invitations."

"I'll just have to remedy that," she told him, disengaging herself from Abe's bear hug. "How about I have you and Sophie over to dinner with Rocky?"

"I'll talk to her. She's out doing some shopping for me this morning." Abe went for the coffee. "Did you hear she's negotiating a deal on a condo in Boca Raton? Wants me to go in on it with her."

Abe paused, seeming to wait for her reaction. Gracie, however, did not know what to say. Her emotions were in a jumble over the situation, so anything she might offer would be tainted by sentimentality.

"Not that she needs me, mind you," Abe went on, apparently accepting her abstention. "Sophie's got plenty of money."

He grabbed the metal cream pitcher with one hand and the coffee pot with the other. "She's outlived two husbands, you know. And Sophie's always had a great mind for finances. She's been in one of those ladies' investment groups for years."

"I remember someone else mentioning that." Gracie told him. "That's where she met Gordon Welty, I believe."

A furrow appeared in Abe's forehead, and Gracie feared his scowl would curdle the cream.

"I haven't met him," she quickly reassured him. "But I've heard enough about him to think you're probably right!"

Abe made a disgusted sound. "He wants my sister to loan him the money to buy *my* place! The gall! He tried to tell me that the day of small delicatessens is over. 'Everything is big, big, big!' he says. Franchises and chain stores are in, because they can buy in bulk, handle more customers in less time, and provide a bigger selection."

Abe waved his arm and plunked the pitcher down with a thud, almost splashing her with cream. "I've invested more than thirty-five years in this business. Thirty-five! I paid a better than fair price for this place, even though the fellow who owned it before was struggling."

Abe reached under the counter for three cups. "This big shot Gordon Welty thinks it's time for my business to go kaput? 'What does he know?' I ask you. He knows how to schmooze the old ladies, that's all he knows. They have names for men like him, but I'm not going to stoop to using them!"

Rocky flashed Gracie a look-what-you've-started look. "Just remember, Abe, it is *your* decision when to sell. The deli's not some white elephant, ripe for the plucking by bargain hunters like Welty, no matter what he would have you believe."

Abe straightened his shoulders. "Abraham Levi

Wasserman will retire when he is good and ready—and not *one* day before. If that means this place isn't worth what I paid for it, then so be it!"

Rocky gave him a thumbs-up.

"You can't take money to the grave, you know," Abe told them in all seriousness. "So what am I going to do with money, if I had it, huh? I don't have children. My niece and nephews are well off. They have more than I do. There is nothing I can give them that they can't afford to buy themselves."

She often entertained the same thought concerning Arlen, Wendy and even little Elmo. They had much materially, so she'd decided to make her gifts love and time. Things had changed since the Depression days of her early childhood.

"You ever see a U-Haul behind a hearse?" Abe was saying. "That's what I ask Sophie when she gets up on her soapbox. She's so caught up in material wealth. It may buy you an expensive bed, I tell her, but it won't buy you a good night's sleep."

"I'm seventy-two years old," Abe went on. "My ruts are comfortable ones. It took me a lifetime to round them out. I don't *want* a new groove. I told Sophie the same thing about my old recliner. Its back fits mine perfectly. I don't *need* a new chair or a new home, thank you very much."

Again, Gracie wanted to give him a furious hug of

solidarity. Arlen and Wendy were always lovingly urging her to update or remodel. Why did no one seem satisfied with *comfortable*?

"A man should do what makes him happy." Abe was saying. "So what if he dies scraping his grill? What will he have missed, I ask you? Nothing. If a man lives a good life, doing for others—being kind to animals and such—"

He looked at Rocky. "We call these good deeds *mitzvot*, 'keeping the Commandments.' Those you better take to heart." He turned back to Gracie and laughed. "And the most important Commandment? 'Do the things your mother told you' should have been included in the Big Ten! My mother, may she rest in peace, used to say this."

Gracie loved her friend.

"Sophie can have her mah-jongg every Sunday night. She can take all those senior citizen discounts at the restaurants, and stuff herself silly. I'm going to be eating off my own plates in my own home until I can't eat any more!"

He shook a finger at them. "And don't you think they'll be sticking any tubes in my veins to feed me. If I can't chew it, I'm not going to eat it."

Rocky timidly offered his coffee cup to be filled.

Abe was suddenly quiet, seeming to have calmed himself. After a moment he continued, "Sophie and Welty say they have my best interests in mind." He paused. "Phooey!" he practically spit out.

"I'll have the special," Rocky requested, this time with his usual force of decision.

Gracie was glad he was abandoning the eggshell approach. Abe was only working himself up into a tizzy that she feared would do nothing but aggravate the ulcer that sometimes acted up on him.

Abe started toward the kitchen, then turned to ask, "Bagel or croissant?"

"Croissant! Since when does an authentic Jewish midwestern deli offer a pantywaist French thing like that?"

"Sophie brought them."

"I'll take a *bagel*."

Gracie ordered kugel. "How is Amy doing, by the way? I hear her family's hosting an Italian exchange student."

"Sweet girl—Maddie, I mean." Abe looked through the serving window. "My mother's family was Italian. Neighbors helped my uncle and his family to escape through the mountains into France. Most Italians did not support Mussolini when he sided with that evil German, may his name be cursed forever!"

Gracie confessed, "I don't know much about Italy and its Jewish citizens."

"Well, it's a matter of record." Abe's tone was matter-of-fact. "Italy deported them to concentration camps."

Rocky attempted a whistle. "So your ancestors were Italian

Jews?"

"On my mother's side. My father's family settled in Chicago before the turn of the century. They were German— very devout." He furrowed his brow again. "I don't know what happened with their grandchildren." Laughing, he added, "We're really not very religious. Agnostics in mind, but Jews in spirit. Most of us are in the synagogue for Yom Kippur—out of guilt more than devotion, I'm sorry to admit."

"It's the same with Christians," Gracie told him. "My dad used to call them 'water, rice and dirt' Christians. They appeared in church for baptism, marriage and burial."

"And you wonder why I don't go to church!" Rocky exclaimed.

She gave him a "gotcha!" look. "Since when have you made decisions based on the opinions and actions of other people? You, the impartial journalist, who is always seeking the truth!"

He dove into the hash-brown potatoes on his plate.

"So tell me about your son and his family," Abe asked, changing the subject. "I hope you brought pictures."

Gracie reached into her waist-pack. "I just happen to have them with me."

Rocky rolled his eyes. "Asking a grandmother if she has photographs is like asking a Jewish deli owner if he has pastrami."

Abe let out a belly laugh, and for the next twenty minutes they enjoyed amiable conversation about her family, Manhattan sidewalks and, above all, little Elmo.

"How is Wendy doing with the new dance studio?" Abe wanted to know.

Gracie was touched that he remembered her concern when Arlen and Wendy were having trouble coming to agreement over her career aspirations—the dance studio, in particular.

"It seems to have worked out," she told him. "Wendy teaches classes every morning while Elmo's at school."

"A very handsome father and son!" Abe picked up a snapshot of Arlen holding Elmo. "In fact, a beautiful family! You are very blessed, Gracie Parks."

She smiled. "That I am."

Abe handed the photos back. "You are quite right to be very proud of them both."

"I worry about them, though. They are so busy—so much stress. The East Coast seems to play at seventy-eight speed." She looked at Rocky. "I said that to Arlen and he didn't know what I meant. He barely remembers the phonographs at all, much less those old records requiring a faster speed on the turntable."

"Your grandson won't know them at all," Rocky reminded her. "We're getting old, Gracie girl."

Abe shook his head. "According to Welty, the neighborhood deli is a thing of the past. Young people want fast service and fancy packaging." He sighed. "And Sophie will tell you I should sell for altruistic reasons: fast food will provide relief for the hectic lifestyle being led by families like Arlen and Wendy's."

They sat in companionable silence. Gracie recalled that Wendy or Arlen brought home take-out food several times a week, even though she'd volunteered to cook while there. But she hadn't thought of New York habits being adopted in Willow Bend.

"Times are changing." She thought out loud the sentiment Marge had so recently voiced. "Maybe we're just stuck in our ways. We've just got to pull over and give progress the right of way."

Rocky took a sip of coffee. "I never was the patient type. And I must say, I'm not sure who has the right of way in this instance. There's something to be said for the wisdom of age."

Gracie nodded. *Is not wisdom found among the aged?* she recalled from the Book of Job. *Does not long life bring understanding?* She smiled, also recalling, *Gray hair is a crown of splendor; it is attained by a righteous life.*

It's still gray underneath, Lord. Will you grant me this vanity?

"We're getting older," Abe reiterated.

"Better," Rocky corrected. "Like vintage wine."

"Vinegar," Abe pointed out. "It sometimes ends up sour like vinegar. I don't want to go sour."

"You won't," Gracie assured him. "We've got each other

to encourage us and keep us accountable."

Rocky smiled. "And think of the combined wisdom of this triad. We've got experience that's sweet enough to temper the most acrid of wine."

Abe nodded, seeming to savor Rocky's analogy. *"The glory of young men is their strength,"* he said, softly repeating the words from Proverbs, *"gray hair the splendor of the old."*

"So take croissants off the menu," Rocky said. "Your bagels are the best. You know your business—stick to it."

"I use the water method."

"I don't care what method you use," Rocky told him. "I care about the guy who makes 'em! Abe Wasserman *is* this deli!"

Gracie lifted her coffee cup to toast Abe. "And he is the sharpest guy I know. A sage among men! A friend above friends!"

"I'll drink to that!" Rocky said, following suit.

Abe beamed.

A GLORIOUS MORNING! The sunrise layered wispy strands of cloud with bands of crimson and apricot. Birds chattered greetings from the trees—and Willow Bend yawned, not *quite* so eager to start the day.

Gracie was more than ready to return to routine and, as she prepared to head off on her morning prayer-walk, one thing she especially anticipated was serendipitous encounters with old friends.

Gooseberry barely opened his eyes when Gracie called him from his windowsill perch. It was obvious that this morning he preferred sunbathing to accompanying her. It was probably all the better, since just his shadow set the birds aflutter and sent the sparrows under the bird feeder into coronary arrest.

Gracie paused to watch. A blue jay rooted for choice morsels in the tray as a sparrow waited patiently below. She could almost see her grandson's chubby finger pointing to the birds in the park, asking her their names. Little Elmo was interested in everything, especially anything that Grandma liked. And Gracie loved birdwatching. Uncle Miltie and Rocky had attached a special feeder to her kitchen windowsill so she could enjoy avian visitors without their seeing her and becoming frightened.

Her grandson had posited the pecking order at the feeders they watched in the park. Pigeons were greedy, blue jays bossy and finches nervous. The little boy had had a soft spot for sparrows—"ordinary birds," he called them.

Gracie could see his reasoning; their mottled brown feathers blended with the autumn landscape as they contentedly foraged for leftovers. She decided that she, like Elmo, had a preference for sparrows. Ordinary birds were like the *ordinary* folks in Willow Bend. They were decent and hardworking, only taking what they earned, sharing all they had. . . .

Gracie popped a southern gospel cassette in the player and donned her headphones. Prayer-walking was good for both body and soul. Well, maybe more soul than body in her case! She pushed on her tummy, as she fastened her cassette player to her pants pocket. Thirty days of her daughter-in-law's healthy organic fare had not made a pound's difference in her weight.

Might as well resign myself to the fact I'm always going to be what polite advertising calls a "fuller figure," she told herself.

Gracie was proud of the fact that she could make the

almost four-mile circuit in just under an hour. She had started the routine years before, working her sadness out on the pavement when El died. And, as time passed, she found herself enjoying more and more this quiet time with God. She remembered fondly that day she felt God match her pace, saying, in His still, small voice: *At last, I have you alone.*

It had been true that her prayer life for a long time was little more than a blessing shopping list. She had come to God with special requests and took little, if any, time to listen. Praise-walking had helped her learn to listen.

Arlen had bought her a portable cassette player not long after she instituted her routine. He couldn't imagine walking an hour in silence. Gracie started listening to gospel music. Occasionally, she would pop in a book-on-tape, but usually it was inspirational music. She'd discovered the words often contained answers to prayers, and the music . . . well, she could almost hear her spirit soar. But there were still lots of days when only silence satisfied the craving in her soul.

This day, Gracie headed down the sidewalk eager to make up for the weeks she'd lost while staying with her son. As safe as the kids claimed their New York neighborhood to be, Arlen was not comfortable with her prayer-walking, so Gracie had contented herself with morning outings to the nearby park with Elmo, asking her Lord to walk along, enjoying the camaraderie.

She loved pushing Elmo on the swing, while answering

what seemed like a million questions about nature, God, family and playground propriety. Often, she could feel God laughing with her at the naive wisdom of a four-year-old. *Let the little children come to Me, and do not hinder them, for the kingdom of God belongs to such as these.*

Gracie added, *They are precious, aren't they? Their faith is untainted by the cynicism of life experience. They are Yours, in all their joy and sympathy.*

Gracie could almost feel her grandson's small hand now slip into hers, as it had all those days in New York. She smiled, recalling him as he expounded on Life According to a Precocious Preschooler.

During their time together, Gracie had taught Elmo a silent exchange of endearment she had used with his father. She would squeeze Arlen's hand three times: *I-love-you.* He responded with a double squeeze: *How-much?* She would squeeze hard. Then they would reverse roles. Little Elmo used both hands, squeezing so hard she would have to beg for release. Her role as mother had been special, but becoming a grandmother was the greatest pleasure of all. How she wished El could be with her to enjoy these days—and his namesake.

She and her grandson had shared many delightful excursions during those weeks together, but experience told her that Elmo would remember longest the *ordinary* times: tea parties with stuffed buddies, building Lego cities, and both of them curling up in his bed with piles of picture books, only to drift off to sleep in each other's arms.

It seemed to Gracie that folks most truly treasured those plain human moments. A gentle squeeze on the shoulder during a time of sorrow or an encouraging word after a disappointment: these were confirmations of all that is shared. And, like sparrows, the Lord's servants thrived best in communities.

Gracie really didn't have time to waste, yet she always seemed to have plenty to spend with the people she loved. Each morning when her feet hit the floor, she joyfully thanked the Lord for the gift of another day, and for all the blessings she was about to receive.

Gracie picked up the pace, humming cheerfully with the tape: *Oh, Sing a New Song to the Lord.*

She stopped to talk to Hallie Finkmeyer, who was watering the chrysanthemums in her front yard. Gracie loved the little bungalow landscaped with evergreens and holly bushes, perennials spilling over their mulch confines. The place reminded her of her own childhood home. Her mother had been a disciplined gardener.

Hallie updated her on the Hadlocks, whose daughter, Suzy, was learning to play the flute. "Linda Cantrell plays, you know. She's giving Suzy private lessons."

Gracie had expected to see more folks out on such a

glorious Saturday morning. Uncle Miltie's predictions seemed eerily correct. Were folks really too busy to enjoy the day? Were they destined to choose prefab nourishment over family fellowship? She hoped not.

She waved to old Mrs. Martin, while making a mental note to check in on Joe and Anna Searfoss. Anna was almost blind, a complication of her advanced diabetes. Joe, her husband and caretaker, would probably relish some encouragement and a meal. She would prepare a supper basket, complete with a casserole and all the fixings for dinner and dessert.

That idea made her chuckle, thinking that that was *exactly* what Gordon Welty was planning to make money doing! Family take-out! She had really been at it already for years, fixing supper baskets for shut-ins, new mothers, the freshly grieving. But there was no way ever to put a price tag on that service, much less on the generous payments she'd received—in friendship and in love.

Gracie was about to turn the loop and head home when she heard, "Gracie!"

Estelle Livett came up beside her.

Gracie slid her headphones to her neck, and greeted the self-appointed diva of Eternal Hope Community Church's choir. Estelle was the only one in their group who'd had formal voice training—even though it had been more years ago than Estelle cared to remember.

"Took your suggestion." Estelle said, panting. "Started prayer-walking—week before last."

Gracie smiled, secretly hoping Estelle was not planning to join her every morning. This was her time for walking alone with only the Lord as her companion—which, of course, meant she wasn't alone at all.

"I'm doing a two-mile circuit," Estelle proudly told her. "But I came this way for a change, thinking that I might run into you. Marge told us last week at choir practice she was picking you up at the airport."

She slowed her pace. "Have a nice visit? How is that grandson?"

"A real sweetheart." Gracie smiled, picturing Elmo's bright smile. "It was a wonderful visit, but I'm still glad to be home." She looked at Estelle, sure the woman wanted more than small talk.

"I was excited to show you what a good influence you've been!"

Gracie felt guilty for suspecting her friend wanted something more. "I'm sure you are going to feel better for it."

"A mile a day keeps the cardiologist away." Estelle smiled. "When my doctor suggested I get some more exercise, I remembered your pep talk on prayer-walking. So here I am! Thought I'd surprise you. Mind if I keep you company?"

Gracie was determined to remain hospitable. "Of course, I

don't mind." How could she? It wouldn't be neighborly—or Christian, for that matter.

Estelle was a bit of a know-it-all who tended to grate on everyone's nerves, Gracie included. *But no matter how crusty a person seems, there's always cream filling hiding inside.* Estelle did, once in a while, prove the truth of the Parks Family Rule Number Five.

"I'd love your company, Estelle," she said, meaning it.

Gracie was about to slip her headphones on, but thought better of it. "I usually listen to inspirational music, gospel mostly."

Estelle wiped her glistening brow with a monogrammed linen handkerchief. "I like arias—classical. One *could* use that as an opportunity to improve the musical ear. I guess if I'm going to do this every day, I'll have to buy one of those contraptions."

I'm looking for that cream, Lord.

"I *do* wish Barb would do a few more classical pieces," Estelle went on. "Music that utilizes more of our talent. You know, dear, I've had years of voice training. But does our choir director employ my talent? *No-oo*, she's infatuated with those schmaltzy praise choruses! We need some *meaty* music! Something classical. Something that will make the congregation sit up and take notice!"

Gracie paced herself to match her companion's slower stroll; but, even after slowing down, Estelle's breathing remained rapid, her face shiny with sweat, as her obviously newly purchased red nylon jogging pants scratched rhythmically. Gracie couldn't help feeling sorry for the woman.

Estelle was a bit more than slightly overweight. But Gracie also fought the battle of the bulge and knew how hard it was to keep within the narrow parameters of those insurance company health charts.

As they headed toward Main Street, she described other experiences she'd shared with her grandson, confessing that they usually napped together every afternoon. "Uncle Miltie and Elmo—it seems I have napping boys wherever I am."

"What do you say we stop at Abe's?" she asked her friend. "I could use an iced coffee."

"Split a danish?"

"A woman after my own heart!"

Amy Cantrell was behind the counter. In front of her sat a petite brunette, whom Gracie presumed was Matilde. "*Buongiorno!*"

Matilde turned to face her. "*Buongiorno, Signora! É italiana?*"

"Goodness no! That's the only Italian I know! I can say *ciao* and *buongiorno!*"

The dark-haired girl laughed with her, and Gracie extended a hand. "I am Mrs. Parks—everyone calls me Gracie. It's a pleasure to finally meet you."

"I am Matilde Bettega. Please call me Maddie."

"I love Amy like a granddaughter." Gracie said as she

smiled at her young blonde friend standing behind the counter.

"We all do," Estelle added.

Gracie thought Amy bristled ever so slightly. Perhaps the girl had not totally forgiven Estelle for the times she had attempted to usurp her solo in the the choir. But Amy was young, and granting true forgiveness took spiritual maturity. And Estelle did have the uncanny knack of grating on everyone's nerves, even those of the most patient saints in the choir loft.

Amy smiled at Gracie. "We've missed you." Then to Maddie: "Mrs. Parks is everybody's *nonna*." And to Gracie. "*Nonna* is *grandma* in Italian."

"I have heard your name spoken often." Maddie's slightly crooked grin was fetching. "You are special to my new sister and her family. I am sure we will be equally as good friends."

Gracie glanced at Amy. Her blue eyes were still guarded behind a slight flicker of lashes. Was there something between these two teenagers?

Amy tended to be a solitary person. She got along with others fine, but seemed to prefer her own company to that of friends. She'd gotten close to Patsy Clayton, the physically handicapped little girl who lived next door to her. But as far as Gracie knew, Amy had few, if any, close acquaintances at school.

That was why it had surprised her to hear that the Cantrells had taken an exchange student. Amy had never expressed any interest, insofar as Gracie could remember. "Are you enjoying your experience in America?" she asked Maddie.

"Of course! This a wonderful country." She smiled demurely. "I am very happy with my host family. And I am especially happy to finally have a sister!"

"You're an only child, too?"

Maddie must have sensed her surprise. "Yes, I am an only child. But the situation is not as you may think. I lived with my grandmother until her death last summer."

Gracie wanted to reach out to the girl. "I'm so sorry."

"Her mother lives in Cleveland," Amy told Gracie.

"We are not close," was all Maddie would offer.

She wanted to ask about the girl's father, but suspected that, too, was a touchy subject. "So who is taking care of you, now that your grandmother is gone?"

"I do not need *anyone* to take care of me." The coldness in the girl's voice unnerved her a bit. "I am eighteen."

"But what will you do when you go back to Italy? Where will you live?"

"I plan to go to the university. I have plenty of money. My grandmother provided for me in that way."

She must have sensed Gracie's surprise, because her tone softened. "Don't worry about me. I do have friends and family in my town in northern Italy. I will be fine."

Gracie wanted give her a hug, but didn't want to overstep

her bounds. Instead, she would pray for the girl. Gracie felt there was sadness lurking behind Maddie's bravado. She and Amy were indeed a curious pair.

"Where is Abe today?" Gracie asked, tucking her impressions away for future mulling-over.

Amy clapped her hand to her mouth. "Oh Gracie, it was terrible. Poor Abe. Hot grease splattered, hitting him in the face. Mrs. Glass took him to the hospital to have him looked at. She called a little while ago, saying he'll be fine and that she was taking him home after they put a patch on his eye."

"I answered the phone," Maddie said. "Signora Sophie said we should watch everything until she can get back."

"How did it happen?" Estelle wanted to know.

Amy pointed to the deep fryer. "Abe was making french fries for Maddie."

"I love them," the Italian said sheepishly.

"They must have contained a lot of crystallized water," said Amy. "That is the only thing we can figure out. He shook the bag into the basket and the grease bubbled up, erupting like a volcano."

"One minute he was joking with the signora, the next minute he cried out, hands on his face! I felt so terrible!"

"It wasn't your fault." This time Gracie reached out to touch her shoulder. "It was an accident."

Maddie shook her head. "If I hadn't wanted the french fries. He got them just for me, you know. The day before yesterday Signora Sophie told him how much I loved them. It was Mr. Welty, who's a friend of hers, who had offered to bring a new wholesale brand."

"I've had frozen vegetables ice up like that, especially if they've had a chance to thaw," Estelle said. "They must have been old potatoes. I think they accumulate the ice crystals when they're left in the freezer too long."

"So when will Abe be back?" Gracie asked, deciding it might be better to stop by his place and check on him herself.

Amy shrugged.

"Signora Sophie did not say."

Gracie planned to call him as soon as she got home.

"You're our first customers today!" Maddie exclaimed.

"Mrs. Glass is concerned about that." Amy sighed melodramatically, much the way Gracie remembered Sophie doing. "You can't run a business on a dozen customers a day."

"Abe seems to have been doing fine for years," Gracie reminded her. She was feeling less and less amiable toward Abe's sister, even though they had known each other for years. Sophie acted as if she loved the deli, and had always baked oodles of delicious breads and pastries whenever she visited. Gracie wondered what had really caused her change in enthusiasm for this place. Florida?

Estelle scanned the understocked pastry counter. "Did Abe ever find his keys? I remember he was hunting for them when I was in last." She looked up. "Do you have any fresh danish?"

Amy's mouth circled in surprise. "He didn't put them out!"

Maddie jumped up and darted to the kitchen. "I'll get them."

"What is this about keys?" Gracie wanted to know.

"He misplaced them the other night," Amy told her. "Thankfully, Mrs. Glass had the spare. Believe it or not, the keys turned up in the freezer."

"The freezer!" Estelle laughed. "Now that's a first!"

Maddie returned carrying the pastries. "It's a big walk-in freezer. But *Signor* Abe swears he didn't put them there. I can see why his sister is worried. He does seem a bit confused."

"Abe *is* getting old," Amy pointed out.

"That is why Signora Sophie wants him to move to Florida," Matilde said. "I understand many old people in America do that, yes? We do not have these retirement places in Italy, so my grandma, she loved the hospital where she had a television and friendly nurses. She would have liked one of those places, I think."

Gracie wanted to tell the children that seventy-two was *not* old. And that not all old people lived in perpetual sunshine. She, for one, had no intention of ever devoting herself to shuffleboard or to scoping out the early-bird specials at local restaurants!

It was Estelle who voiced her opinion. "Maddie, Abe

Wasserman still has a lot of productive years in front of him. Let's not put him out to pasture in Florida just yet. He told me that he has no intention of retiring."

Maddie started to say something, then reddened with chagrin.

"*Thirty* is old to children," Gracie said to Estelle. "Remember how ancient we thought our parents were? Age is relative."

Estelle laughed. "Yes, I suppose you're right. I glance in the mirror and see who I want to see. I get up close and the truth ambushes me. When did I get all these wrinkles!"

Gracie smiled at Maddie. "We oldsters get a bit defensive on age-related issues. You see, most of us are quite active, and intend to stay that way for a very long time. The thought of not being able to contribute to society is scary."

"I'm, ah, sorry," Maddie said sweetly. "Nonna was also active. She worked in her garden until her last months. She loved herbs, and provided all kinds of medicines for people in our village. She was quite famous for her natural remedies."

Gracie was intrigued. "I use them to cook, but I don't know much about herbal medicine."

"I could teach you!" Maddie looked pleased.

"What can I get you, Gracie?" Amy asked, taking the tray from Maddie.

Estelle looked at her watch. "I don't think I have time to split that danish, after all. I hope you don't mind—I forgot that I'm meeting Barb Jennings before practice tonight, and I have to drive over to the Christian bookstore in Mason City and pick up music to preview."

Gracie was looking forward to seeing her fellow choir members and their director that very night. "I forgot, the ecumenical program is in a few weeks, isn't it?"

"Three, to be exact." She looked at Gracie. "Maybe you can join us, and help me talk our stubborn leader into doing something more sophisticated!"

Gracie wasn't sure their group was ready for that. Some weeks, simple harmonizing seemed complicated enough.

"How about it, Gracie?"

Barb would need moral support, that was for sure. Estelle could be obstinate. "Sure, I'd be happy to."

"See you this evening, then, before rehearsal."

But Gracie was thinking already about her other old friend. Abe, too, would also need an advocate.

GRACIE ARRIVED AT THE CHURCH before Barb and Estelle. The sanctuary had a timeless feel, with soft emerald light streaming in from the windows onto well-worn oak. It seemed to invite seekers to come and sit a spell. The century-old building had been adopted by the Eternal Hope Community Church in the early sixties when the Presbyterians moved. She and El had joined right after moving to Willow Bend.

The Parks Family Rules held that *The best place to solve a problem is usually alone with God in a warm, cozy kitchen*, Gracie knew. But today she might just amend it to: *The best place to tackle a problem is alone with God in a quiet, familiar choir loft.*

The creak of her footfalls on the steps was like a welcome greeting. She found a spot in the loft, bowed her head and began sharing her concerns about Abe, Sophie and Gordon Welty with the Lord.

Abe had sustained second-degree burns—one was to his eyelid, irritating the tear ducts. He told Gracie on the phone that he looked like a pirate, with a patch over one eye. "A freak accident," he called it, none too convincingly. Gracie wondered if Abe was beginning to doubt his own capabilities.

What can I do to encourage him, Lord? You and I both know Abe must not lose confidence in himself.

Gently lowering her head to listen, she soon heard something unexpected—a soft sniffling. It was Amy in the front pew. Gracie looked heavenward for encouragement, then moved to greet the girl.

"Oh, Gracie, I've made a mess of things again!"

Gracie sat down beside her. "There, there, it can't be anything you, me and God can't solve together."

More sniffles.

She handed Amy a tissue and waited for her to gather her composure.

"Maddie and I had a big fight. She wants to go home to Italy! She hates me."

"Oh? You two seemed happy enough this morning when I saw you at the deli."

Amy shook her head. "We're not getting along at all. She

hasn't liked me almost from the first day. My parents think she is wonderful, just perfect. They think I'm exaggerating—that I'm jealous of her. She's so charming to everyone, with her accent and everything."

Gracie had to admit Maddie seemed beguiling, but couldn't help wondering if the girl was as wholesome and wholehearted as her charm led them to believe. There was something hidden there, in her spirit, that Gracie intuited and found worrying.

Amy herself had recently been through a lot emotionally. But she was strong. And she had a heart of gold. Nevertheless, she was still a teenager, and they had a tendency to be melodramatic.

"I hate myself for feeling this way," Amy said as she blew her nose. "Maddie does try to be friendly."

Gracie rubbed Amy's back, but didn't reply.

Amy looked at her with imploring eyes. Gracie pulled the girl into her arms.

"What exactly does Maddie say?"

Amy stiffened. "Nothing specific. It's weird."

Gracie held her by the shoulders to look into her eyes. "It must be hard sharing your family—your life—with another person. You've had your parents all to yourself for so long."

"No! I *wanted* her to come." Amy brightened. "I was really looking forward to this year. I've always been fascinated with

Italy, and I thought it would be fun to learn the language. They only teach Spanish, French and German at school.

"When they asked for host families at school, I was completely excited. When I saw her photograph in the pack, and that she was from Italy, I knew she was the one for us. Her English is great."

She looked at Gracie. "Maddie even wanted specifically to come to the Midwest. I think Chicago or Cleveland—yes, Cleveland, because her mother lives in Cleveland."

"But she said she doesn't see her."

Amy shrugged. "I thought it was strange, too. You know, she went home with Mrs. Glass last weekend. She wanted to see the Rock and Roll Hall of Fame."

"And her mother."

Another shrug. "She didn't tell me, but I don't think so."

"You two don't talk much."

"Not really. School stuff mostly. But she gets along fine with Abe and his sister. She likes my granddad, too. And your Uncle Miltie. We have that in common." Amy's smile was endearing. "We both like you grands."

Gracie smiled her gratitude. "We grands, as you call us, like you, too. Uncle Miltie is smitten with both you girls!"

"He's so funny. I love his jokes."

Gracie shook her head. "Don't tell him that, or there'll be no living with the man!"

"Thing is, Gracie, somehow Maddie's always making me look bad. She jumps to do what I'm supposed to be doing. She does my chores—things I planned to do—but she does them first."

Amy leaned back in the pew. "She always apologizes— even praises me and gives me the credit. But that makes me look even *worse* in front of my parents. It looks like she's covering for me! And if I say anything, it seems as if I don't appreciate her, or that I'm being petty."

"Have you talked to your parents about this?"

Amy nodded. "They try to be understanding, really. They say Maddie is only looking to find her place in our family, and that I should make an effort to be a little bit more accommodating."

"Seems like sound advice."

Another nod. "Maddie does the same thing at the deli. I think she wants my job. She's always volunteering to do things for Mrs. Glass. Maybe I *am* jealous. I think secretly she hates me."

"Emotions can be deceiving. We have to interpret them with common sense and lots of prayer." She squeezed Amy's hand. "There is also something to be said for intuition and hunches. What you may be sensing is jealousy—in *both* directions."

Amy looked puzzled. "What are you saying?"

"Don't be so hard on yourself. You can't always control how you feel, but you can control how you behave. Your parents are right, Maddie needs a good friend. This *is* a different culture, and she must be particularly vulnerable, considering what she has been through."

Amy sighed. "I know you're right. I'll try harder with Maddie."

"Do you want me to talk to her? Just to form an opinion of my own?"

Amy's expression was tentative.

"I won't mention our conversation."

Amy nodded, and Gracie gave her another hug.

"Well, well, well!" Barb Jennings scurried down the aisle, Estelle close behind her. "Gracie Parks in the flesh!"

Barb hugged her with one arm, since the other was loaded with sheet music. "It just hasn't been the same without you!"

"I've missed you all." Gracie meant it with all her heart. Why did the people she most cared about have to live so far from one another?

It was an awkward moment. Barb was not the demonstrative type and fidgeted with the stack of music in her hands. "Estelle and I are looking for something for the ecumenical service."

"She told me." Gracie gave a side glance to Estelle. "She invited me to your meeting."

Barb looked at Estelle. "The objective voice?"

"We can't let Waxman Tabernacle get all the accolades this year," Estelle replied tartly. She gave that superior smirk for which she was famous.

Barb made a disgusted face for only Gracie's eyes. Eternal Hope's choir director didn't handle intrusions on her turf very well.

"It's amazing what we can accomplish when it doesn't matter *who* gets the credit," Barb said before Gracie had a chance to gather her thoughts. "We can't all be stars, Estelle. Our church is small. Perhaps we're meant to be supporting choristers."

Gracie decided diplomacy would be the order of this meeting. She signaled a truce with her hands. "I understand this is an ecumenical presentation. Barb is right, we're all working together. Estelle is the one in our group with formal training, so I'm sure she's taken our voices into consideration in picking out music. Let's sit down and look at what you both have found."

"My sentiments exactly." Barb spread the booklets and tapes out on the pew.

Estelle uncrossed her arms, relaxing a little. "I just don't want to do some *ordinary* piece from years past."

Ordinary. Why did folks have to say that word with such disdain? Gracie resisted the urge to share her grandson's philosophy on sparrows.

"We are looking at new pieces, are we not?" Barb's voice

still had an edge to it. She shoved what was left of the stack toward Estelle. "You picked up the preview music, saying you checked out almost the entire sacred music section of the Christian Light Bookstore."

Estelle did look like she was acquiescing, but Barb went on. "We have a limited vocal range in the choir, and Rick Harding has hinted that this is a busy time for him." She glanced at Amy, who seemed to be trying to blend into the pew. "Amy is the only other outstanding soloist, and she's got both her school work and job at Abe's to consider."

Now Estelle was miffed.

"Let's have a look at our options," Gracie said, trying to diffuse tension.

Amy leaned forward. "I really shouldn't get a big part," she said timidly. "Barb is right, I may not be able to give the time needed for practice. Mr. Wasserman hasn't been well, so I've been working more. And with school and everything, I'm feeling crunched."

"Thank you for telling us that, dear," Barb said. "We appreciate your loyalty to Abe. How is he? I heard about the accident."

There were very few secrets in Willow Bend. Their lives were just so intertwined, it was hard to distinguish where family ended and community began.

"He's okay," Amy told them. "Mrs. Glass called me. The burns were serious, but manageable. He says he'll be at work tomorrow bright and early."

Amy glanced at Gracie. "Maddie, our exchange student, has also agreed to help out. I've got a big test in physics day after tomorrow, and a paper to write for English."

"Ah, Maddie!" Barb looked at Gracie. "She can sing, too! Amy brought her to practice." Back to Amy: "Why don't you see if she would like to join us? With the two of you sharing responsibility at Abe's, it just might free up enough time."

Amy looked at Gracie as if to say, "See what I mean?"

Gracie smiled at Amy. "We would like you with us. There would be a gaping hole without you."

"I'd like to do it. I don't want to let anyone down." She glanced tentatively at Estelle. "But I don't know if I'll have time to practice something special. So I think I'd like to just be one of the supporting voices."

"Well, we'll see what we can do." Barb was in control now. "I've found a few selections here that seem to complement our talent. Some of it is classical, probably a bit more sophisticated than we are used to." She glanced amiably at Estelle and added, "No one can say Eternal Hope is not progressive. We're up for the Lord's leading."

They decided on a richly melodic piece accompanied by a

flute, which Gracie remembered Amy's mother just happened to play. Linda Cantrell was not only the school librarian, but also was an accomplished flautist, who had played in a community orchestra in Florida and had won awards in college. Amy seemed pleased at Gracie's suggestion that her mother accompany the piece.

Gracie offered to ask Linda the next day, knowing how reluctant the woman usually was about extra commitments. Gracie also hoped to have a little chat about her daughter and a certain Italian exchange student.

Gracie eased her Cadillac, Fannie Mae, in behind the van parked on the other side of the street from the Cantrell house.

Lord, please give me wisdom.

"Buongiorno, Signora Parks." Maddie greeted her at the door, and her welcome seemed heartfelt.

"Is Mrs. Cantrell at home?"

Maddie invited her into the living room. "She'll be here directly. She called to say she was picking up some things for dinner, and that was over an hour ago. But she was coming right home. You can wait if you like—or perhaps *I* can help you?"

"Is Amy here?"

"No, she's doing some research at the library. She has a big paper due soon. But really, signora, I would love to have you stay." Maddie ushered her into the living room.

"You're not working at the deli today?"

"Signora Sophie decided not to open up, to give her brother another day to recover."

Gracie chose the armchair by the fireplace. "Perhaps we *can* chat—get to know each other a little better."

"I'd like that."

"Well, tell me about your perceptions of America, now that you've been here a while."

Maddie sat across from her. "It is very interesting here. In some ways, it reminds me of home. But it is so flat!" She smiled. "I miss my mountains."

"I've seen photographs. The Alps are quite beautiful."

They sat in silence a moment before Gracie asked, "Have you been to the States before?"

"No."

Another awkward silence. Gracie nodded, trying to decide on another topic for discussion.

"I have visited Germany," Maddie offered. "France and the British Isles, but, yes, this is my first visit to America."

Gracie repositioned herself, moving the pillows. "Is it what you expected?"

"More or less." Maddie shrugged. "We know a lot about America—television, movies and music. American culture, it has overtaken the world, I think."

Gracie felt her way gingerly. The image portrayed was probably not too flattering. "Hollywood is hardly representative of America."

"Probably not." Maddie agreed. "Sometimes I feel, ah . . . like I am in a movie. It seems . . . how do I say? *Weirda*? Weird is the word, yes?

Gracie nodded again, enjoying Maddie's Italian accent.

"I am here in the center of all I have seen in the movies. I arrived in America in New York City. It was familiar, but also alien. Very strange for me. I cannot describe this feeling. It is like you know something, but you can't possibly know this."

Gracie had probably experienced something similar when visiting Arlen. New York City was probably almost as alien to her as it was to Maddie. Gracie felt so removed from Arlen and Wendy's life.

She remembered lying in bed and listening to the city that did not sleep. Oh, how she had missed the night music of Willow Bend, the chitter of crickets and frogs! She looked at Maddie, this other stranger in a strange land.

"I used to hear American music and not understand all the lyrics." Maddie smiled. "Imagine my delight to finally know what it is they are saying! Amy likes to hear what it was I thought they were singing. We have much funny with this."

Grace chuckled, more at Maddie's choice of words than the story. Her English was almost impeccable, and delightfully softened by her lilt. Gracie took that opportunity to ask, "Your mother is American, right? Has she lived here a long time?"

"My mother is Italian. But yes, she has been here since I was a little girl. I do not know her very well."

"That is sad."

A shrug.

"You said Amy's mother—Linda—would be home soon?" Gracie looked at her watch. Uncle Miltie would be wondering where she was.

Maddie nodded. "They are good people. Linda is very kind to me. She tries to make foods I like, so I am sure she is looking for some ingredient from the Italian recipe book she bought."

"You are very lucky to have them for host parents," Gracie agreed. "Isn't it wonderful you and Amy came together? You were both only children, and now you're sisters!"

"Yes, this is very special also to me."

"You and Amy are about the same age?"

"She is younger. I was eighteen in June."

"But still, you have a lot in common."

Maddie chuckled. "Hamburgers."

"*Hmm?*"

"Amy loves them. I did, too, when I first arrived. *Basta* hamburgers! Enough already!"

Gracie was intrigued. "Funny you should mention that. You know, there is quite a controversy going on in town over whether or not Willow Bend needs a fast-food restaurant."

"We have only McDonald's, in a city near my little town. It is popular with young people, but families do not usually eat meals there. This is a surprise for me in America. I never imagined so many fast-food restaurants, and that people eat there so often!"

"Uncle Miltie would like Italy."

Maddie cocked her head.

"He considers fast food a family nemesis." The girl stared, perplexed, so Gracie explained Uncle Miltie's philosophy on home cooking and the family dinner table, admitting she had to agree with him. It seemed families had gotten much too busy to enjoy one another.

Maddie didn't comment, but seemed sympathetic.

"There's a fellow looking to launch one of those take-out supper places in our town."

"Mr. Welty. The friend of Signora Sophie. Remember, I told you that he brought the french fries. He was in the store—how do you say—the night before the day?"

"Last night," Gracie told her.

"Yes, the last night before this one. Signora Sophie gave him a tour of the deli, and he suggested Signor Abe get a new freezer. He used to sell them, you know."

Maddie paused, seeming to study Gracie. "He seems concerned for Signor Abe." Gracie said nothing

"I like the deli. It reminds me very much of Italy. We have small places like this. We don't shop so much in supermarkets as you do. I am glad that Signor Abe does not want to sell it."

Her expression turned doleful.

"I did not mean offense with what I said about old people and Florida. Truth, I think my nonna would have liked such a place. A home in a warm place when it is cold, and a familiar home for the summer.

"In my country, many people go to the beach or the mountains in the summer months, so to have two homes is not so unusual. Often, one is an apartment. And many older people travel much, but my nonna never did. I think, ah, she regret it."

Gracie smiled, appreciating the girl's openness. "We didn't take offense, dear. I have not traveled a lot. As a matter of fact, I recently returned from my first trip to New York City, so I can identify with what you just said about feeling *weirda*."

Maddie chuckled, obviously enjoying Gracie's teasing.

Just then they heard Linda come in the back door, calling to Maddie to retrieve the rest of the groceries from the van. Linda appeared in the doorway. "Gracie! I wasn't expecting you!"

Linda asked about her time at Arlen's, and Gracie went on to explain the idea for the ecumenical concert, telling her about Barb's choice of music featuring flute accompaniment. Thankfully, Linda was flattered.

"Roy has been after me to get involved with music again, so I agreed to take a few students."

"Suzy Hadlock."

Linda was dumbstruck. "How did you know? She's not only my first, but she just now had her first lesson!" She grinned. "Oh yes, you have your ways. Gracie Parks, Willow Bend's own Jessica Fletcher!"

"I prefer Miss Marple."

They laughed together.

Linda took the seat opposite her. "I used to play rather a lot when we lived in Florida, but that feels like eons ago. I've been so busy with my job at the library, and getting Amy settled in our life here, I haven't had time to think about me. I've wanted to get more involved in the church, it's just that Amy has needed me."

"Then this will be the perfect opportunity."

Linda's smile was timid. "I'm really rusty."

"Nothing practice can't remedy."

"Oh, but the time! I can hardly accommodate what I do now!"

It was Gracie's turn to smile. "Choir practice always starts and ends on time. Punctuality is next to godliness in Barb Jennings's mind. Besides, it's something you and Amy can do together."

"Lord knows, we need that." Linda sighed. "Teenage mood swings—will I be able to endure it, Gracie? Amy can be *so* trying. And now, with the two of them. . . ."

Linda glanced toward the kitchen, where Gracie guessed Maddie was putting away groceries. She lowered her voice. "We'd thought taking an exchange student would be a great experience, Amy being an only child. But she's terribly jealous. We've had such a time with her. Really, Gracie, Maddie is being a peach about the whole thing. I don't know what to do. I hate to tell the agency that it isn't working out."

"It *is* early in the year, after all," Gracie pointed out, opting not to betray Amy's confidence. "The girls probably just need time to adjust to the relationship. Like you said, Amy has been the only child for a long time—and so has Maddie, I take it."

Linda nodded. "Yes, I'm sure you're right. We've told Amy as much, but she has her own issues. I suppose all parents of teenagers voice similar concerns.

"But sharing this musical experience with my daughter should be a treat. And it might even ease the jealousy problem, since they'd be spending more time apart. Maddie loves the deli, and Amy might be willing to cede more time there to her once she has this added responsibility."

Gracie prayed Linda was right.

5

GRACIE ARRIVED HOME to find Uncle Miltie and Rocky in the garage, with the automatic garage-door opener on the workbench in what looked like a thousand pieces.

"What are you doing!"

Rocky harrumphed. "The man won't listen to reason."

"It can be fixed!"

"Hogwash! The fellow at the hardware store said as much. The motor is shot! Face it, man, and buy another!"

Uncle Miltie waved his screwdriver. "That's the problem with folks today! They think everything is disposable! Disposable lighters, razors, napkins—everything's a whim away from the landfill! Whatever happened to good old American durability?"

"Durability is one thing, George Morgan. Plain old stubbornness is another!" Rocky turned to Gracie. "How long have you had that opener—eighteen, twenty years? I remember El having trouble with it and threatening to buy another. That was ten years ago, at least!"

Grace raised her shoulders and palms in submission. This was one argument in which she was not going to get involved. Her darling uncle was on a mission to be helpful, and she was all for humoring him. He had fixed the umpteen thousand problems that El never had time to address. Her darling husband had been a handy man at many tasks, but not when it came to home repairs.

The garage-door opener was the least of them. The door had hung up at the three-quarters mark as long as she could remember. Thankfully, it allowed Fannie Mae just enough clearance to barely graze the radio antenna.

"You boys battle this one out on your own." She reached for the doorknob. "I'm going to fix supper. Rocky, you want to stay? I've got a chicken *cacciatore* simmering in the crock pot."

The newspaperman grinned. "I got a whiff of it when I arrived. I was hoping you'd invite me."

As she pushed open the back door, the argument between the two men was in full swing again. Rocky was fond of her uncle, of that she was sure, but the two of them bickered like magpies.

As she added seasoning to the chicken, she thought of Maddie and sent a prayer heavenward, asking God to work in the hearts of both children. *A dash of prayer helps any recipe. ...*

She added Arlen and Wendy, while she was at it. And Estelle? She had a tough crust, that was for sure; but it seemed God wanted Gracie to see the tender filling inside.

I'm sorry for judging, Lord. I often look only on the outside— You, Father, see the heart. Thank You for giving me Your eyes so that I can better appreciate what lies beneath.

Rocky sopped the last of the sauce on his plate with a wedge of bread. "You outdid yourself this time, Gracie, my girl. I love old-country dishes, and cacciatore is one of my favorites. Simple fare, but soulful for an Italian boy."

"I hadn't thought of you as Italian."

Uncle Miltie arched his bushy brows. "*Gravino* isn't exactly Anglo-Saxon."

She put her hands up helplessly. "I guess I was thinking of Rocky as more American than, say, Maddie. I forget sometimes we all have foreign roots."

A snippet of an afternoon spent with Arlen and Elmo in New York Harbor came to mind. "I was so proud to read the words on the base of the Statue of Liberty: *Give me your tired, your poor, your huddled masses yearning to breathe free ...*"

"*Send these, the tempest-tossed, to me,*" continued Rocky, and she finished with him. "*I lift my lamp beside the golden door.*"

He closed his eyes for a moment, apparently reflecting on those immortal words. "My grandparents came to America through Ellis Island. One in every ten Americans has Italian roots, you know. We strengthened the backbone of this country. . . .

"My *nonno* worked construction all his life for *Sogno Americano*—the American Dream—a house in the suburbs with a shiny red sedan in the driveway."

"Did he get it?" Gracie asked, enjoying his reminiscence.

Rocky nodded. "However, it was seeing his first grandson graduate from college that gave him the greatest joy. He bragged about it all the rest of his life.

"And it was one of the greatest moments of my life, too. I can still see him standing beside my parents, applauding until his hands must have hurt. Nonno's grin was worth more than all the awards I took that day!"

He looked at Gracie. "He's been dead twenty-five years, and I still miss him."

Uncle Miltie reached over and patted his friend's hand. "Thank the Lord for heaven! We'll all be together someday."

Gracie rose to get the dessert. "How about a cup of coffee and dish of raspberry sherbet?"

"Got any cookies?" Uncle Miltie wanted to know.

She felt a tinge of guilt, admitting, "I haven't had a chance to bake."

"Why, you just got back, my dear!" Uncle Miltie pushed his

chair away from the table. "I didn't expect homemade. There's a box of vanilla wafers in the pantry. They'll do just fine."

Rocky pushed his chair out to stand. "You relax and let me fix dessert. I know where everything is."

He opened the cupboard and retrieved cups. "So, what do you think of our international guest? Maddie seems like a sweet girl."

"Yes, she does." Gracie watched Rocky as he reached for the sugar bowl. He did know her kitchen almost as well as she. She especially wanted to tell him how thankful she was for the time he spent helping Uncle Miltie. Rocky's agility and strong arms brought back-up to her darling uncle's desire to be helpful. Gracie knew it must have been Rocky who disabled the malfunctioning garage apparatus in the first place. And he would be the one finally to mount the replacement.

"Maddie's had a difficult life," Gracie told him, refocusing on the conversation.

Rocky leaned against the counter. "Another foundling for you to nurture?"

"Maddie seems pretty independent to me," Uncle Miltie called from the pantry. "She doesn't seem the type that needs mothering."

"I don't know about that," Rocky said, pausing a moment. "You should see her with Sophie. I think she misses her grandmother a lot more than she cares to admit."

"I think her grandmother left her a pretty hefty inheritance," Uncle Miltie added. "At least that's what Abe gathered from a conversation he had with her."

"She hinted as much," Gracie confessed, remembering her conversations with the girl, and sensing the emotional tempest that might well lie behind those startling blue eyes. "I think our little Italian is very lonely. I think that she's been terribly disappointed, and she's perhaps a bit shy. Probably afraid of getting hurt again."

"Hey, look what I found!" Uncle Miltie put the plastic container of Marge's leftover cookies on the table. "Well, you'd know, Gracie. You've always been a keen judge of character."

Rocky flashed a roguish smile. "Willow Bend's sleuth for all seasons."

Grace accepted the compliment with a meek smile. "Woman's intuition."

"I suppose," Rocky conceded.

"So, did you also get a chance to talk to Abe? I heard he had another mishap."

"What happened?" Uncle Miltie immediately wanted to know.

Gracie filled him in on the accident with the splattering grease.

Her uncle eased himself back into his chair. "His sister may be right. I've known folks a lot younger than Abe to develop Alzheimer's, or some other kind of dementia. Even

I'm not as sharp as I once was." He let loose with one of his famous guffaws. "Why, at my age, my mind wanders all the time—it's just too decrepit to wander far, that's all!

"But, Gravino, I can still whup you at chess without working up so much as a mental lather." He laughed again. "And I'll have that garage-door opener working as good as new!"

"Harrumph!" Rocky swatted the air. "You, Professor Morgan, have had a run of good luck, that's all. And as far as that old opener is concerned, I say, put your money where your mouth is!"

Uncle Miltie hooked his thumbs under his suspenders and leaned back in his chair. "Even a blind pig gets lucky once in a while and finds an acorn in the mud!"

Rocky wrinkled his nose, and Gracie just shook her head.

"I called Abe today," Gracie told them. "He's actually raring to get back to work. I'm not surprised. I think it was just an accident, that simple."

Rocky shook his head. "Abe did seem a little off his usual sharpness when I last talked to him. He'd mislaid his keys, insisting someone had taken them and claiming he'd never misplaced them in more than thirty-five years of doing business."

Gracie was embarrassed to admit, "They were in the freezer."

Her uncle almost choked on his coffee.

"Where?" Rocky stared incredulously.

She hated to repeat it. "In the freezer."

"And you think he's okay?" Miltie shook his head. "Gracie, *normal* people don't put their keys in the freezer."

Rocky was more sympathetic. "It's a walk-in. Abe has the key to it on the ring, so it isn't *so* far-fetched."

"I suppose," Uncle Miltie conceded. "None of us wants to admit we're slipping. But Abe's lucky he has folks who care."

Uncle Miltie glanced at Gracie, his expression revealing his appreciation of her continual concern for him. "Abe's sister seems willing to invest in the future, not knowing where that may take them. Seems to me we ought to support Sophie in this. She obviously wants what is best for him."

Gracie wasn't so sure, but decided to keep her opinion to herself.

An agitated Sophie called the next morning, just as Gracie was getting ready for Sunday school. "Abe is missing! We had an argument early this morning and he stormed out. I went to the deli to make amends, and he wasn't there!"

"It's only half past eight," Gracie said, glancing at her watch. "Perhaps he went for a walk."

A sigh. "My brother opens his place at eight o'clock sharp. But long before that he's got the day's baked goods in the oven. He left this morning on schedule—half-past-five, the same as he's been doing for as long as I can remember. I gave him plenty of time to calm down, so I didn't leave for the

84

deli until seven. He's not here yet, Gracie! And I'm worried!"

"Are you alone?"

"The girls are here—Amy and Maddie. I called them to cover in case we have to go looking for him." She paused. "I already called the hospital—nothing. I hate to call Herb Bower. What do you think?"

Gracie closed her eyes and sent up a prayer on Abe's behalf. "I think we need to stay calm, give him a little more time before we panic. He may have gone for a walk and returned home after you left."

"I called. No answer." A long pause. "Gracie, I said some awful things."

Although this was no time for lectures, Gracie longed to give Sophie Glass a piece of her mind. Abe was a grown man, generous, thoughtful and wise. He didn't need his sister managing his affairs. And he certainly wasn't mentally incompetent.

"I'll take a detour by the park, call you on my cell phone if I find him," she told Sophie, remembering that Abe sometimes took over leftover crusts and crumbs to feed the birds and squirrels. "Why don't you make a pot of your mother's chicken soup? He may need it."

Abe was sitting on a bench, pitching pieces of roll to the sparrows, when Gracie found him.

"*Ordinary* birds." She sat down beside him. "That's what my grandson calls them. He likes them because they share with each other, and don't take more than they need."

Abe nodded, breaking off another bit of the bread he was holding, and crumbling it onto the ground. "Sophie sent you to look for me? She thinks I need a baby-sitter."

"She's worried."

"Sophie was born worried."

Gracie smiled. Abe loved his sister, of that she was sure. Sophie showed up at the deli on a regular basis, always ready to help out, and usually bearing new recipes they could try together.

"I don't want to talk about it," he said.

Gracie folded her hands in her lap.

"Don't try to force me."

She wouldn't.

"The woman is impossible!"

Gracie nodded.

"There's nothing wrong with my mind, I can tell you that. I'm as sharp as a tack!"

"I know."

"What do you want to do?" She surprised even herself with her question.

Abe looked at her. "Bake my strudel. Sell bagels. Pour coffee. Listen to people tell me their problems, and share their joys. I don't want to do anything that I am not already doing. Does that sound so strange?"

"Not at all."

"I don't want to sell, Gracie."

"Don't."

"I admit—I'm not getting any younger. I do forget things. Perhaps it's better if I sell while I can get a good price. It needs a lot of remodeling, you know, and not just the kitchen."

"But the fifties look is all the rage!" she told him. "Why, Arlen took me to a place in New York with chrome and red enamel tabletops, just like yours! They had the same padded chairs—reproductions! Arlen says they pay a mint for the stuff we might think is dowdy."

Abe smiled. "You're a good friend."

"So are you."

"You heard I left the coffeemaker on—burnt dry. Could have caused a fire. You know about the keys, and the hot grease. I locked myself out of the store, too."

Gracie didn't know what to say.

"I couldn't remember my mother's maiden name. God rest their souls, they were Italian Jews. I wanted to tell Maddie about my family and I couldn't remember—can you imagine? I could *not* recall the name of my mother's family!"

She squeezed his hand, holding back tears.

"I'm seventy-two years old. Never married. Never even seen the ocean. I always wanted to do that, Gracie. Go to Atlantic City—walk the boardwalk, buy saltwater taffy."

"Why didn't you?"

"Never found the time." He looked past her, perhaps

reliving earlier times. "The deli has been my life. Time goes so fast—when you're not even looking." A half-hearted chuckle. "I must have gotten old then, too, because I don't recognize the man in the mirror. Not that I was a looker. So, maybe it's not so bad. Wrinkles or acne, who can say which is worse?"

That made her smile. "You still have your sense of humor."

He squeezed her hand. "Life is tragic. You have to laugh . . . or you cry."

"Always the pragmatist."

"Cultural hazard." He chuckled.

"You can still go to Atlantic City," she told him, not wanting to comment on his observation. "Seventy-two isn't old. I've read they're thinking of pushing the retirement age back to seventy. Our kids probably won't see Social Security before they're your age or older."

He shrugged. "Welty says he'll keep my name on the window. And the place will still have my Chicago deli look. Maybe I should sell."

"Sounds like you are feeling sorry for yourself." She narrowed her gaze. "Where is the determined man I talked to the other day? You were spitting mad!"

"The other day I hadn't almost killed my sister."

Gracie felt her jaw drop.

"Yes, that is what I did. But she won't tell you, I'm sure. She has a prescription that must be refrigerated. I put it in the cupboard. Why I put in the cupboard, I don't have a clue. I put away the groceries she bought, and we were talking. I knew it had to be stored at a certain temperature. She's been taking it for years—always reminds me.

"Thankfully, we got the pharmacist to drop off a fresh supply."

"It was an oversight, Abe. It could happen to anyone."

He shook his head. "I haven't misplaced my keys in thirty-five years. I've never locked myself out of the store. Why didn't I look for ice crystals on those potatoes?"

"Because you're human. You care about people. Your mind was probably on Amy or Maddie or one of the umpteen people who come to you for advice every day."

"I am worried about that girl."

"Amy?"

"Maddie."

She looked at him for an explanation.

"She has a hard heart. I can see it in her eyes."

"Windows to the soul," Gracie said, repeating his wisdom.

He smiled. "There's hurt there, too, Gracie. She won't talk about her family, but she'll tell you all about the lake by her home, and the geese. She feeds the geese here, like I feed these pigeons and sparrows. She talks to *them*, when she should be sharing her heart with loved ones. She's not so different from me. Hard heart, true, but it's a good heart. I know the condition."

She hugged him. "Two hard-hearted softies."

He relaxed in her embrace.

"I understand Maddie has gotten close to your sister."

"She went home with Sophie to see Cleveland, but didn't want to visit her mother. Sophie offered. The mother doesn't live more than a stone's throw from my sister, but Maddie refused. Made some excuse about her mother needing more notice. She didn't even want to call her."

Gracie decided to share what she knew about the relationship between Maddie and Amy, sensing that redirecting Abe's concentration might take his mind off his own problems.

Abe nodded. "I noticed the tension between the girls. Maddie has started coming in more and more by herself. She looks forward to Sophie's company. Says it reminds her of her grandmother, while Maddie is the daughter my sister never had. She raised three sons, you know. God bless her!"

He looked at Gracie. "You might want to tell Sophie about the tension between the girls. My sister is hard on Amy."

Gracie asked why.

"Amy and I work well together. She gives me a wide berth, knows what I want to do myself. I'm fussy about some things. Maddie is more apt to go ahead without checking with me first. To Sophie, this is being more industrious. I tried to tell her that the girls are just different, that Amy understands my idiosyncrasies and is only respecting my preferences."

He rolled his eyes. "But you know my sister, she makes a big deal—a mountain out of a molehill. 'Sophie, Sophie, Sophie,' I tell her, 'leave the girl alone.'"

Abe made a motion to stand. "You going to take me home, or are you going to make this old deli owner walk?"

"First, I'll give Sophie a call—tell her the lost is found."

"I don't even own an answering machine."

She stared at him quizzically. "That came out of nowhere!"

"I was just saying. So many new things, so many changes. It gets confusing. Truth is, I didn't want to have to figure out how to use the blasted machine."

Sticking the rest of the bread in his sweater pocket, he said, "For later. God sent manna enough for one day. Our daily bread. The birds that missed out can wait until tomorrow. Me, I'm going to the deli to make chicken soup."

"I think Sophie is already ahead of you on that one."

ARRIVING AT CHOIR PRACTICE a few days later, Linda and Amy pulled into the church parking lot just ahead of Gracie and Marge. As they walked into church, Marge asked, "Where's Maddie?"

"She went to a meeting for all the exchange students in the county," Amy said.

Linda slipped her arm through her daughter's. "They get together once a month and plan special trips. Right now they're sharing ideas for getting involved in their communities. The organization encourages them to do that."

"It would be great if they could do something here," Marge said. "We can always benefit from a little cultural exchange."

"I was thinking an international dinner might be fun. A

potluck night." Amy said. "During youth group, we talked about hosting a Third World craft fair. Remember my telling you about it, Mom? There's an organization that sponsors them, and all the money goes back to the village crafters."

Linda was excited. "I thought it was too grand a project at the time, but if the kids got involved...."

And if we center it around food, Gracie thought, chuckling to herself, *we're bound to get a good turnout!*

Marge's eyes brightened. "We could get our guests to share a little bit about their different cultures. I could decorate with flags from the different countries. I saw them in one of my catalogues."

"Maddie would cook something, I know. She loves to cook for us." Amy looked at her mother. "I think the others would, too. I've met most of them, and they all seem nice. I'm sure they would want to participate."

Gracie was thinking out the logistics. "Would the kids be responsible for running the craft fair?"

Linda nodded. "I'll make a few phone calls to the parents on the youth advisory board. Amy, you can bounce it off Pastor Paul and then discuss it with your friends. As for support from the host parents, tell him to leave that to me."

"We'll ask Maddie about it tonight when she gets home," Linda told Gracie. "The area representative will drop her off, so I could talk to her, too. I'll say it's tentative, see if there's any real interest."

As the four of them neared the other waiting choir members, they quickly mentioned possible dates, publicity, and responsibilities. Gracie was pleased to see Amy taking a lead; she seemed confident, and Gracie understood the responsibility would be good for her.

As Linda headed to the piano to work with Barb, Gracie motioned Amy aside. After complimenting her on the idea, she asked, "Are things better between you and Maddie?"

Amy lowered her head. "There's one part Mom didn't tell you about tonight. Maddie wants to live with Abe and Sophie."

"But Sophie lives in Cleveland! She doesn't usually stay in Willow Bend more than a week or so."

"Abe needs her now."

Gracie didn't comment on that.

"Maddie and I are getting along, though, probably better than we have since she got here. I think we've worked things out somewhat. She loves helping out at Abe's place, and it gives us time apart. I've needed time to concentrate on tough assignments, and work on this concert for church."

"So why does she want to move?"

Amy just shrugged. "She says we'll still be friends. It might be better, really. We won't get on each other's nerves."

"And this is all right with Abe and Sophie?"

"I don't think she's asked them yet. She wanted to see if it would be okay with the exchange agency first.

She talked to me about it today before she got picked up."

Barb waved them over from the piano. She was really excited about the new piece and convinced Eternal Hope's choir could turn out to be the hit of the performance. She was beginning to sound like Estelle!

Estelle beamed when Barb thanked her for having been so persistent about previewing new music. When Barb complimented Linda, Amy hugged her mother. Gracie was doubly proud of the part she had played in something that was turning out to be so exciting for everyone involved.

Uncle Miltie was still fiddling around with the garage-door opener when Gracie and Marge got home from choir practice. Rocky had long since given up, swearing he was going to buy Gracie a new one, just for spite.

"Remind me *not* to call your uncle if anything at my house breaks." Marge scanned the workbench, awash in tools and parts to the opener. "My first husband used to take things apart. He couldn't get them back together, either. I sold boxes of that junk in my yard sale. Guys like you scarfed it right up."

"Never know when you might need a washer or pin just this size," Uncle Miltie said, holding up a greasy metal rod. "This is the piece causing all the trouble. Problem is, they don't make replacement parts for it any more."

He eyed Marge. "And if you hadn't sold that stuff of your husband's . . ."

"You wouldn't have been able to find the right needle in that haystack of junk, anyway." Marge laughed. "Come on, George Morgan, admit it. Gravino was right, you're going to have to bite the bullet and buy a new opener for Gracie."

"*Phah!*"

Gracie sighed, wondering how long it would take her dear elder relative to face the truth. She really didn't want to park in the driveway all winter! A door that opened three-quarters of the way was better than one that didn't open at all.

"Gracie, any of that apple crisp left from dessert?" Uncle Miltie washed his hands in the utility sink. "A man thinks better on a full stomach."

Marge teased. "You mean he eats better on an empty one! A perpetually empty one!"

"You watch out, or I'm going to come next door and fix *your* garage-door opener! Maybe I'll just discover your pin fits snugly in *our* opener!"

Marge gave him a playful jab. "You keep your tinkering confined to your own side of the hedge!"

"Did you hear about the man down at the Willow Mart?" Uncle Miltie asked.

"What man?" Marge wanted to know.

Gracie, however saw it coming and ducked into the house first.

"A case of root beer fell on him," he said loud enough for

her to hear. "But don't worry, he didn't get hurt. They were *soft* drinks!"

Marge jabbed him again. "I'm heading home, Gracie. Charlotte probably misses me. She takes her nightly stroll around the backyard about this time, and I wouldn't want an accident."

"You know what dogs and telephones have in common?" Uncle Miltie demanded. Before Marge had a chance to tell him that she didn't want to know, he zinged her with, "*Collar I.D.*—get it?"

"Oh, please!" Marge headed back to her house, shaking her head.

"By the way," Uncle Miltie said, following Gracie into the kitchen, "Rocky was right about Welty buying the Carruthers place."

Uncle Miltie took one of the chairs and sat down at the table. "He's not only checking out the deed, but he also hired a lawyer."

Gracie decided then and there. "I have to meet this man. Is he staying at Cordelia's?"

"Don't rightly know." Miltie spooned some ice cream on the apple crisp she set in front of him. "He goes back and forth to some place near Chicago, I know that. He's got a restaurant there."

"He's from Cleveland, right?"

Uncle Miltie shrugged, concentrating on the bowl of gooey dessert.

Gracie fixed herself a cup of water for tea and put it in the microwave. "I'm going to stop by the deli and chat with Sophie."

"It's going to rain tomorrow." He looked up, a drop of ice cream sticking to his chin.

She dabbed her napkin to get it. "I really did miss you."

"And me you, Gracie girl." He smiled. "I was thinking of calling my son. He's always dogging me to visit. It's probably about time I did. He said he'd come get me."

Uncle Miltie always put off that trip, claiming he didn't want to be a nuisance; but Gracie suspected he was embarrassed by the walker. Uncle Miltie's son and his wife had grown children, and traveled a lot. His grandchildren weren't married yet, and led busy lives of their own.

"They'd love to have you, I'm sure." She reached to take his hand. "But I'd miss you."

He squeezed hers. "I know the feeling."

The following day it rained, just as Uncle Miltie had predicted. It wasn't just a drizzle, but a cold, steady rain, the kind that chills to the bone. Gracie wore a wool sweater, but she still couldn't get warm. She hated to turn up the thermostat, so, instead, she decided an afternoon of baking was in order.

"I'm planting a bug in Cordelia's ear about Gordon Welty's buying the Carruthers place." Marge had come over to keep Gracie company. "She'll find out what's really going on."

Gracie slid a pan of brownies into the oven. "Don't do anything until after I talk to Sophie. I'm going to see if I can maneuver a way to meet this man."

"He's a smooth talker, Gracie." Marge rolled her eyes.

"Abe called him a '*schmoozer.*'" She chuckled. "I, for one, *like* to be schmoozed once in a while."

Gracie was feeling a little guilty about judging a man she hadn't met. "Anyway, Marge, he might just be all he seems. We really don't know for sure what he's doing."

"No one is *ever* all he seems," Marge reminded her.

Gracie thought of Maddie. She would talk to Sophie about the girl's desire to switch homes. "You're right, Marge, no one is as he seems. Or she seems."

"Except maybe *you*, Gracie."

Gracie batted her eyelashes.

"And you thought I was in New York visiting little Elmo! Didn't it ever occur to you I might have a secret life as a Rockette?"

They both giggled.

"Speaking of surprises, how about Estelle and Barb?" Marge shook her head. "I never expected our defensive choir director to admit that our arrogant diva could have a good idea."

Gossip, like the brownies in the oven, was decadently delicious, but it could betray even the closest of friends. That was another problem with small towns—everybody knew everyone else's business. Choir loft prattle seemed innocent, but Gracie knew that was only an illusion.

"Well, that only goes to show that there is hope for us all," Gracie answered. "Estelle and Barb working together can only be good for the performance. I'm looking forward to this ecumenical event. We sounded wonderful last night!"

Marge smiled. "We did, didn't we? Linda and Amy are big assets. I must admit, I was hoping Maddie would join the choir, too. She has a great voice. She sang with us a couple of times while you were gone."

"Perhaps God wanted it this way. It's nice that Linda and her daughter can share this experience. Amy seemed so much more relaxed, confident really."

Marge agreed. "That was a great idea, to try to set up an international fair. I hope we can make it work."

The future was beginning to offer several perfect opportunities to mend fences. Amy and Maddie would have occasion to work together. They might discover, like Estelle and Barb, that a project gets done more efficiently when it doesn't matter who gets the credit.

Gracie decided to walk to Abe's and found she couldn't have planned it better, for who was sitting at the counter?

None other than the man she was seeking, Gordon Welty. Marge was right, he virtually oozed charm. If she hadn't been warned, she might even have been taken in by his suave manners and genially flirtatious style.

She guessed him to be nearly her contemporary, but it was hard to gauge exactly. In questioning him, she discovered he wasn't currently married, although he was cagey as to whether he ever had been. Gracie decided it wasn't worth pursuing.

"So you run a catering business," he said.

She only nodded.

"Gracie's the second-best cook in Willow Bend," Abe called out. "I am too modest to name the best."

Sophie was scrutinizing an invoice. "You canceled the order for frozen croissants?"

"My homemade bagels are fine," Abe told her.

"Croissants are popular," Welty told him.

Abe stepped out of the kitchen. "Not with me. I've had plenty of requests for my bagels—none for croissants. I use the water method, you know. None of this convenience stuff for me. I make them like my grandfather did, may he rest in peace."

Sophie straightened. "He was also my grandfather."

"He loved the *old* ways." Abe smiled smugly. "You used to love them, too."

His sister put her hands on her hips. "But the man was progressive! He knew the future of the delicatessen was in take-out. Remember, he was the first one to sell cold cuts. And he was the first one to sell bottled pop.

"You, Abe, you get caught up in your homespun psychology. Leave it to the bartenders, I tell you! People are in the right frame of mind for receiving advice then. They can ignore it after the hangover—if they can even remember that long. Or give the business to my son, the big-shot psychiatrist!"

"Sophie, I don't want to fight with you." Abe's tone was gentle. "But you know as well as I, our grandfather cared about people. Mama set the same example. She always had time for folks. Always doing for others."

He stepped closer to his sister. "You are a lot like her, you know. You take good care of Mike and me. We don't appreciate you nearly enough."

Sophie noticeably softened. "You stretch yourself too thin, Abe. You work long hours. You never take a vacation. You run the risk of a stroke or heart attack. I worry about you."

He brushed the air. "You worry about everything, Sophie. My mind is good. What can Florida offer me that is better than this?" He took in the counter with a gesture of his arms. "I have good friends—a home—in Willow Bend. And Gracie tells me the fifties are back in style!"

Welty cleared his throat. "But everybody deserves leisure, Abe. You've worked hard all of your life. Now you're entitled to treat yourself." He looked right at Gracie. "All your friends want you to reap the benefits of a productive life, isn't that right, Mrs. Parks?"

"Seems to me he already is." She smiled at Abe. "He's one of the town's most respected citizens."

Sophie sighed. "Respect doesn't pay the bills."

"I do all right." Abe was indignant. "If this wasn't a lucrative business, Mr. Welty wouldn't be interested."

Welty didn't respond.

"Just what exactly *do* you want?" Gracie wanted to know. "Abe's Deli, or the Carruthers place?"

He stared at her patiently. "I'm following a business plan that requires a few typical American communities to prove my idea is right on. The franchises cater to urban areas, and need high volume to succeed. I figure if my stores stay small, specializing in a few family favorites, I'll be able to launch more of them. Willow Bend seems like just the place. Whether it's this deli or the Carruthers place doesn't matter. Abe's, of course, would require a lesser outlay of capital." Welty gave a grin in the direction of the older man. "And it does have a certain charm.

"But, if Abe doesn't sell, there are other places. He'll just miss a good opportunity. I've offered him a more-than-fair price." He directed a smile at Sophie. "For the sake of my favorite investor."

He turned to Gracie. "If Abe decides not to sell, I'll buy the other property and tear it down, put up something more to my specifications. The place is a firetrap, a hazard to the community."

"You *do* know we have a code that applies to our historical homes?" Gracie asked him.

Welty's expression was smug. "The Carruthers place is not seventy-five years old. Your town codes apply to older places. The house may imitate the style of Victorian architecture, but it wasn't built until 1928. So legally I can buy it and do anything I want with it."

"We also have a code pertaining to macadam." Gracie told him.

Another smug smile. "But there's none governing driveways. This will be a *convenience* place, remember." His expression turned sympathetic. "But I don't want to foist something upon the good people of Willow Bend that they don't want. I think we can work together on this. I only want what is good for the community as well as myself."

"Have you spoken to our town council about your plans?"

He nodded. "Indirectly. Mrs. Stefano and I have had conversations. She's all for it, by the way. I just have to nail down the details."

"They say the devil is in the details," Abe muttered, returning to loading the pastry case. "I'm not selling."

"That's your decision," Welty said. "I respect that." He pointed to the muffins. "I'll take one of those."

Gracie decided the same. Unfortunately, it was too salty to eat. Abe had apparently substituted salt for sugar in the recipe.

ABE LEFT THE RESTAURANT obviously upset, yet insisting that he would be okay. Gracie held a salty muffin, struggling not to race after him. She understood his need for privacy. If Abe really was having health problems, he needed time to be alone, time to pray.

Instead, she offered to help Sophie finish preparing the kitchen for the next wave of hungry people. Welty politely excused himself, claiming to have business in a nearby town.

Sophie was blunt. "I love my brother, Gracie, but something is wrong. I phone him every week like clockwork. I try to visit every couple of months. Abe and Mike are close, but I'm the one who pulls them together. I keep us a family. When Mama died, I just stepped into her shoes. I do what she did all our adult lives. She urged us to call one another, not to forget birthdays, to offer a hand in whatever was needed in the family at the time."

Gracie noticed tears in the woman's eyes and stepped closer to comfort her. "Papa went first, but Mother comforted us when we should have put our arms around *her*. She took over his business, and also helped Mike get started. She was there for Abe, too. I was busy then, raising my boys."

Sophie stopped, and it was obvious that she felt herself assailed by memories too difficult to share. "Did you know I had a stillborn daughter? I wanted to name her after my mother. Rose. Rose Wasserman. I miss my mother terribly, Gracie."

Familiar grief welled into Gracie's throat as she remembered the experience of losing parents. She decided to try to ease the woman's pain by sharing, "El was home when I got the call from the visiting nurse telling me about my mother. She simply drifted off to sleep in her favorite chair and didn't wake up."

Sophie inclined her head toward Gracie, and they stood together in intimate silence for a moment.

"I hung up the phone," Gracie continued, "and El put his arms around me, and I cried and cried. Not for Mother—she was eighty-five. She'd simply been called Home. I was crying for *me*."

Gracie took a step away, so she could look her friend in the eyes. "I was crying because I was nobody's little girl anymore. I simply realized that there would be no going home anymore. I wouldn't have Mother or Daddy anymore to hug me and give me good advice."

Sophie nodded. "Do you have brothers or sisters?"

"I had an older brother. But Buddy died of a heart attack. My mother outlived him. That was especially hard on her."

A smile deepened the lines around Sophie's mouth, and the fine wrinkles at the corners of her eyes. "Abe calls me the quintessential Jewish mother. 'Always fretting, Sophie,'" she said, imitating her brother's voice. "'No need to worry about tomorrow, for tomorrow will take care of itself.'"

Gracie laughed. "I can hear him saying that."

"I've seen him age." Sophie's expression turned serious. "Not so pronounced until recently. He's had some health problems. It's not just Jewish mothers who obsess. The deli isn't doing as well financially. That's what I sense. I think underneath that bravado he's worried he won't have enough to retire on. I wonder if the worry hasn't aggravated a condition that has been slowly progressing."

She met Gracie's gaze. "Maybe you don't notice it the way I do. I hate saying this, because we're all getting older. He's my brother, for goodness sakes. But we have to face facts. Most of us forget things. I bought one of those blasted beeping rings because I was always misplacing my keys."

Gracie searched her mind for some clue, some hint that Abe's mental health had been deteriorating. Her own memory was not what it once was, that was true, but where did a person draw the line? What should one attribute benignly to aging, and when was forgetting cause for alarm?

Abe didn't want to retire. Gracie loved him and understood that. He was also part of the tissue of her life. His sister was looking for an advocate that Gracie couldn't be. She drew back from the next words, but knew they had to be said. "Perhaps you *are* worrying too much, Sophie. Until now, Abe has seemed fine to me."

"You probably think I am pressuring him to move with me to Florida."

Gracie stood quietly, not sure how to respond.

"It's not the reason, you know. I can be happy anywhere, and frankly, I've got the money to buy the condo myself. It's not about finances—it's about my brother. It's *now* that concerns me."

Sophie moved to the other side of the counter. "Abe and I have always been close. I'm his little sister, it's true, but I've been looking out for him for years. Somebody needs to give Abe permission to quit. Gordon Welty is right. He's entitled to enjoy his golden years. That's what this is about."

Gracie couldn't argue with that, but she couldn't help thinking it wasn't what Abe wanted, no matter how much other people wanted it for him. "You said he feels pressured—maybe it's just *time* he needs. He may agree with the move to Florida, but it needs to be *his* decision. He told me himself he always wanted to see the ocean. I think he needs some space to figure out what is best for him."

"Welty offered him a fair price."

Gracie said nothing.

"But you don't want Welty's modern deli, do you? Does anybody in this town care what is best for my *brother*?"

Gracie met those indignant violet eyes. "We care very much." She would not voice now her thoughts about Welty— those were better left for later discussion. Instead, she let her empathy show on her face. "Just give him the time and space he needs, Sophie."

"I've been trying." Sophie's eyes filled with tears again. "But there've been all these incidents . . . there may not be time."

That was one possibility Gracie did not want to face.

Sophie tossed the last of the salt-flavored bread into the garbage. Gracie followed her lead, and picked up the tongs to rearrange the muffins and danish pastries to fill the space in the display case. She didn't want to talk about this subject anymore, so she broached a new one. "Maddie has certainly taken a liking to you."

"A darling girl." Sophie brightened. Obviously she, too, was glad to take the discussion in another direction. "Abe probably told you our mother's family was Italian."

Gracie nodded.

"Italian partisans helped them to escape to France, you

know." Sophie bent to retrieve a box of napkins. "They came to the United States a year or so after the war ended, and lived with our family for quite awhile. My mother's brother and his family, that is. My uncle was fluent in German, French and English, so he worked with the United States military during the reconciliation process."

"So you and Maddie share history."

"Her grandfather died for the cause of Italian liberation. He was a 'righteous gentile,' as we called those who helped the Jews. He cared about his neighbors, particularly those at risk for extermination. Some of our family remained in Italy, and I, for one, am thankful to the Italian partisans who protected them."

Gracie made a mental note to stop at the library and pick up some books on World War II, maybe something on Italy. Next to mysteries, she loved historical fiction. But now she needed some real historical background. "Until Maddie came, I hadn't realized how many people have Italian roots."

She thought out loud. "More than an ocean divides us. I was just a child during World War II, and Europe seemed worlds away. The United States is such an enormous country and such a powerful one that we have the tendency to think we are the world. Having international guests probably helps us to get a better perspective. I'm glad the Cantrells took an exchange student."

They stood arm in arm, admiring the old place. The white enamel refrigerated cases in the fluid fifties style, with rounded edges that seemed softer, more inviting, than the modern, angular models. The padded red vinyl seats of the barstools sat on chrome legs.

But it was the restaurant's front window Gracie loved best. The words *Abe's Deli*, in black lettering trimmed with red and white, spread in a grand arch across its top. There were posters for all the community events decorating the lower panel. Abe's Deli was important to her all right, and she did not want to lose it.

"Leaving this place will break his heart," Sophie said, seeming to read her mind. "I want to be here for him. I want to do right by him. If I thought it would make a difference, I would move here permanently and help him run this place."

She looked at Gracie. "I've raised my family. I've been looking forward to retirement in a nice sunny community in Florida. I have friends there. I like mah-jongg."

Gracie could only smile. Florida's beaches could be awfully tempting on those snowy January days. Gracie wasn't very fond of the blustery March rains either, even if they meant spring was around the corner. They chilled her to the bone, bringing on twinges of arthritis, that emphasized her feeling of getting older.

And she, too, wanted what was best for Abe. Even if that was . . . retirement. Could his mind really be slipping? She didn't like to consider that possibility.

"You know, Maddie wants to live with you and Abe," Gracie said, changing the subject again.

Sophie faced her. "I wondered. Maddie's hinted, but hasn't asked me. I sense something between her and Amy."

"But you're not staying in Willow Bend long-term, are you?"

"I'm staying until we get some answers. I made Abe an appointment for a checkup. I'll stay for as long as he needs me.

"I'm putting my house in Cleveland up for sale. I don't need a place like that for just the summer months, so I plan to sublet a small apartment closer to my son."

"So you would be willing to stay and keep Maddie until the end of the school year?"

"She hasn't asked me. And, of course, Abe and I would have to talk about it. If things aren't working out with Amy . . . well, then, I guess we would take her in. I love young people. They have so much energy."

Gracie sensed Sophie, like herself, also liked feeling needed. She debated whether to say more about the relationship between Amy and Maddie. "Has Maddie admitted she's having problems with the Cantrells?"

"No, on the contrary, she says she likes them. But Amy's

parents are busy. Maddie's used to spending time with older adults. She lived with her grandmother in a small village. She just likes being with Abe and me—I think we're comfortable for her, that's all."

Gracie looked up as Rocky walked through the door.

"Hello, ladies. Is Abe here?"

"He went home, we think," Gracie told him, still feeling a little guilty for not following him to make sure he was all right.

Over coffee, Rocky unfolded what he'd learned from a contact at the local registrar's office. Welty had, indeed, been nosing around and had asked for the name of a lawyer.

"What do you think he's looking for?" Sophie wanted to know.

Gracie ran her finger around the edge of her cup, considering the possibilities.

"According to my source, Welty was looking through the old deeds. He made a few copies." Rocky gulped a last swallow of coffee. "So where can Gracie and I catch up with Abe? I want to see what he thinks. Does he have an encumbrance on this place or something?"

"He's been here for thirty-five years." Sophie's tone was slightly indignant. "He doesn't owe anyone anything." And softening, she added, "Except the the Good Lord. But that loan came with a lifetime mortgage."

"You don't want to go with us to talk to your brother? I

think it would mean a lot to him to know you are on his side."

Sophie shooed them with a hand motion. "Let my brother think what he wants. We know each other well enough. Actions speak louder than words. I'm needed here now to feed his customers and, for all my talk, I know that's what really means the most to him." She grinned conspiratorially at them. "I'm going to make a fresh pot of coffee."

As if on cue, two men walked in the door, sat down and picked up menus.

As Rocky folded himself into the front seat of his little black sedan, Gracie slid into the passenger side, thinking as she always did how outsized her friend seemed in such a small car.

"You know," Rocky said, drawing her back to their conversation, "this whole thing with Abe has hit a little too close to home."

She glanced his way. "How's that?"

"I've got a couple of insolent pups on the staff who think they know more than their ancient editor. They're always second-guessing me. I know they think I'm not as sharp as they are. Oh, Gracie, I hate getting older!"

She didn't mind aging. Each decade brought blessings of its own. Sure, she wished her body didn't creak like the stairs leading to the choir loft at Eternal Hope. But over all, she was happy with things as they were. Each day held the promise of a matchless experience, one that was best appreciated in the light of what had come before.

"You ever wonder if your life is important?" Rocky asked. "Suppose you found out you only had a day to live. What would you do with it?"

She didn't know. So she closed her eyes and tried to imagine. "Maybe I'd have a tea party with little Elmo. I'd invite Arlen and Wendy and tell them how much I loved them all." She smiled. "I'd probably invite you, Uncle Miltie and Marge, too."

"That's nice." He was quiet for a minute. "Suppose you only had an hour?"

She laughed, realizing, "I'd probably just make another pot of coffee, like Sophie did this afternoon."

T HE CHOIR LOFT WAS ABUZZ! It looked like they were going ahead with International Night. The Eternal Hope singers planned to lead a program combining American hymns with several selected by the exchange students. Estelle was pushing for the choir to learn praise choruses in several languages.

But Gracie's mind was on the conversation she'd had earlier that evening with Ann O'Neill. She was not only a town councilwoman, but a lawyer—Gordon Welty's lawyer, in fact. He had wanted to know about an "action to quiet title," something Ann explained was used when there was a deed complication that the buyer felt could not be reconciled. She was not at liberty to share more, but did say that Welty's case was for the moment only hypothetical.

"Earth to Gracie!" It was Marge in her face. "What do you think we should do? Cater the meal and sell tickets, or make it a potluck dinner?"

Gracie refocused in time to see her friends staring, expecting some answer to a question she had missed.

"I like the idea of catering it," Linda said. "We could talk to the foreign students about helping, or at least providing recipes. And we could all pitch in to help Gracie—if she's willing to do it, that is. We could create a dinner with a real multicultural flair, something we couldn't achieve with just a potluck."

She smiled, surveying the group. "And perhaps, if all of us donate, we won't have to sell tickets. Then, people can use their money to buy more handicrafts. We're not that far away from the holiday season, so I think it could really work out well for everyone!"

"So let me get this straight," Estelle said. "Village cooperatives create these handicrafts to be sold through various ecumenical organizations and churches. They act as distributors for these Third World entrepreneurs. So when we sell the crafts, the money really does go back to the craftspeople."

Linda nodded. "That's how it works. I guess you've just elected yourself chairperson of advertising! That's a perfect description for posters and the newspaper."

Happily, Estelle seemed flattered, and agreed to take on

the project. Pragmatist that she was, however, she demanded to know: "We're not going to get stuck with the merchandise, are we? We can send back what we don't sell, right?"

"That's the way it works." Linda assured her.

"I'm for providing a buffet," Marybeth Bower said. "We'll divide up the responsibility and the cost, so the proceeds go to the crafters." She turned to Gracie. "What do you think?"

Gracie couldn't see a problem. "If everyone is going to help. We all go in together to buy the groceries, and we all work in the church kitchen. I think it sounds like a great idea!"

"All settled." Barb clapped her hands. "Thank you, Amy, for suggesting it. I'll give the recommendation to Pastor Paul for approval."

Barb sought Maddie's attention. "Will you talk to the other visiting students in the area to see if they would like to help with the meal?"

"I already have. We think it sounds exciting! We would each love to make one of our traditional dishes."

Maddie looked at Amy. "If it is all right with you. I know this is your church and your idea."

"Of course." Amy dipped her gaze.

Gracie sensed some emotional tug of war was still going on between the two teenagers.

Marybeth spoke up and suggested that they pray. Gracie was thankful for that. Who could argue with prayer? And prayer had a way of easing strain, helping folks to put things in better perspective. Gracie prayed silently for Amy and Maddie, while Marybeth prayed aloud for their project.

Lord, Gracie prayed, *we're never short on ideas around here, and You're always guiding us as we enact them. This one celebrates the thrilling diversity You've blessed us with, but I know that a little world such as Willow Bend is as diverse in its own way as the bigger one these wonderful students represent. And for that—for Abe and Sophie, for Rocky, and, yes, for Estelle, too—I thank You. Also, whatever about us that we think of as* normal *may seem* foreign *to our new friends: help me remember that foreignness is only a state of mind, not being.*

Gracie had just turned the corner on her way to the library when she saw Gordon Welty coming out of the Carruthers place with Carol Whitefield, the real estate agent. She eased Fannie Mae in behind his imported sports car. He watched from the front porch, perhaps fearing she would nick the bumper.

She patted the steering wheel. "Good girl, resist the urge." Her elderly Cadillac probably handled better than that slick little thing of his!

Getting out, she grabbed her umbrella. The rainy weather was causing her joints to ache, particularly her knees.

"Hello, Mrs. Parks," Carol called. "Sorry I can't chat, but I've got another appointment in just a bit." Reaching for

CHURCH CHOIR MYSTERIES

her car door, she stopped her hand in mid-air. "Unless you wanted to talk to me about something in particular?"

Gracie waved her on. "No, I'm headed across the street to the library. I wanted to talk to Mr. Welty, though."

"To what do I owe this pleasure?" He glanced at his watch. "I'm running a bit late, also, but I've got time before my next appointment."

"With a lawyer?" Her brusqueness surprised her.

His smile suddenly wavered, then disappeared altogether. "I don't see how *my* business is any of *your* concern."

"I suppose it isn't," she apologized. "I'm just concerned about my friend. Abe is under a lot of pressure to sell the deli. I think it's affecting his health."

"Or his health is causing the pressure." Gordon Welty seemed to look right through her, his smile cold. "Your friend may be aware that his faculties are beginning to deteriorate. That would be good reason for distress."

"I should think that's for a medical doctor to decide."

Gracie offered a chilly smile in return. Even if she couldn't quell her dislike, she could control her response. She would be polite, nothing more. But it went against her nature to be frosty, so it was an effort.

"Willow Bend is a small, close-knit community. We look after one another. We care about our town and its future. We have town meetings to iron out problems. Everyone seems

120

to know everyone else's business. We mean well, but we can be a little overwhelming to newcomers."

She looked him in the eyes. "I'm not sure an absentee entrepreneur would feel comfortable in our cozy fishbowl."

"Thank you for the advice, Mrs. Parks." He didn't quite meet her steady gaze. "But I'm already feeling quite at home in your little town. Why, I may even have unearthed some old roots."

"What kind of roots?"

He offered his manicured hand. "Good day, Mrs. Parks. Give my regards to Mrs. Glass when you see her. I'm headed back to Cleveland for a couple of days. Tell her I'll contact her the first of next week."

Gracie chose a comfortable wing chair in the library reading room. Resisting the familiar lure of the mystery section, she picked several books on Italian history during World War II, and on the partisan Resistance in particular.

The Italian partisans had been a politically diverse group. Yet they were every one of them determined to rally their countrymen to stand up to Fascism, and later to drive the Nazis from their country.

In the early years of Nazi occupation, the partisans stood alone, for Italy was tired of war, and Hitler did not yet seem so terrible. However, as the Nazi stranglehold tightened, the

Italians balked and the rebellion grew stronger. Thirty-five thousand Italian resistance fighters died for the cause of freedom. Often, the Italian partisans liberated their cities ahead of Allied troops; and they did it by sheer will power, defeating the Germans against impossible odds.

Gracie was looking over a book of photographs of Italy, when she looked up to see Maddie standing in front of her.

"Buongiorno, Signora Parks. I see you are reading about Italy!"

Maddie bent over the color map on the facing page of the book Gracie held in her lap. "That is where I live," she said, pointing to the mountainous area north of Milan.

"Do you mind?" She held her hands to receive the book. Gracie handed it to her, and Maddie sat in the adjoining chair to flip through it. There were many photographs of the lakes and surrounding countryside at the foot of the Alps.

"I am ashamed to say I don't know much about Italy."

Instinctively, Maddie looked at her; then she broke into a smile that lit up her lovely tan skin and accentuated a coppery sprinkling of freckles across the bridge of her nose and cheekbones.

A very pretty girl. Gracie wanted to tell Maddie how attractive she was when she smiled, but felt the girl might misunderstand. She focused her attention on the pages of the book instead. "Beautiful. It looks like just such a beautiful place."

"Yes, it is. You are interested enough to read about my country. That touches me deeply." She slid the book around so they could share it. "Here is Milano—follow my finger—here is Lecco and the lake—and here would be *my* town. It is too small to be on the map, that does not matter. We who know it understand that nowhere in Italy is more beautiful."

At last, Gracie felt comfortable with the child. Maddie had relaxed her reserve, and when her voice lightened, she sounded like the happiest of teenagers, with only joy to share.

"Tell me about your life there."

"Oh, Dorio is the loveliest home—everything about it!" Maddie sighed, almost as if she were traveling home in her mind. "I cannot describe the sunset there or the moonshine without feeling like I am writing silly romantic poetry. Words are not adequate to describe the tranquility. Many afternoons, I sit and gaze on the vineyards terracing our foothills, which stretch down, almost dipping into the blue crystal lake. The breeze is sweet with grapes and sunshine."

She glanced at Gracie, who smiled, letting her expression reveal her vicarious pleasure. Maddie flipped the page to another panorama. "You walk up on the mountain, and you feel like you're approaching the top of the world! It looks a lot like this. The air is crisp and clean! And you sleep as never before. When you wake up in the morning, you are warm and at peace, for in front of you is the silent lake. It pulls you into a dreamy, seemingly imaginary world, yet it is more real than *any*thing you have ever experienced. Dorio does not belong to this world."

It was Gracie's turn to sigh. "You make it sound perfectly glorious!"

Maddie's blush was almost as pretty as her smile. Gracie found herself charmed. No wonder Sophie loved the child. She wondered if Amy had experienced this vulnerable side of her Italian "sister."

"Signora Parks, Dorio has another side, too. Many young people say that Dorio is dead. There is nothing you can do there. There are depressing bars full of worn-out people watching soccer games on a television, smoking, and swearing in uneducated dialects."

Maddie paused, her expression revealing disdain for the opinions of her peers. "They do not spend time in Dorio because they say there is no life. Everybody is looking for the day he'll be able to drive or get a ride to another place . . . anywhere other than the village they think they know."

"It can be the same here, Maddie." Gracie's eyes rested on a photograph of the beautiful Italian scenery. "We have no mountains, to be sure. There aren't even hills in this part of Indiana. But there *are* crisp, cool streams, and lovely glens and forests full of wildflowers and ferns.

"Willow Bend is as beloved to me as I sense Dorio is to you. Young people often leave here, too, seeking adventure in other, more alluring places. They seem to find this place provincial—boring, as you said."

Maddie nodded, seeming to savor their rapport. "They are looking for something they cannot see that they already have! Young people move away from Dorio as soon as they have the means. Perhaps someday they will know what they have traded, and come home. . . ."

There was a longing in her tone that made Gracie wonder if Maddie was thinking of her own mother, hoping *she* would one day return to Dorio. Gracie had entertained that thought often enough about Arlen. He, too, had found Willow Bend two sizes too small for his aspirations. Although she didn't begrudge Arlen his career, and she was proud of him, she understood Maddie's sentiment. Some things were not worth the trade.

Gracie squeezed the girl's hand. "Perhaps they will return someday. They will miss what you and I have come to treasure."

A wistful smile. "I hope you are right, signora."

Another squeeze. "*Gracie*. Everyone calls me that. But I must admit I like signora."

"Okay, Signora Gracie." Maddie squeezed back. "For now, I will accept reality. At the end of a night's adventure in the city, our young people return home, to be wakened early in the morning by church bells . . . only to face another monotonous day in Dorio."

"But not you. I sense you like those bells."

"I am not typical. I loved my nonna and her Old World ways. I respected her herbal medicine, and honored all of her superstitions. I loved her for them. She had only me, you know."

"No, I didn't know." Gracie braved, "I did hear that your mother lives in Cleveland."

"Oh." Maddie, a certain expression working its way to the surface of her face, then said, "My mother and I are not close. She was one of those teenagers who could not be happy in Dorio. Her heart was oceans away, with an artist who came one summer to paint our lovely landscape. But he left her pregnant."

Sensing an uncomfortable quiet start to spread, Gracie searched her mind for some safe response, but it was Maddie who broke the silence. "No, signora, my mother never married that lover. Her husband is an American businessman. The only thing he has in common with my father was nationality."

Gracie didn't want to pry, so remained silent, allowing the love she felt to envelop them.

"My mother left me with Nonna Ida when I was six. She hated Dorio, so she worked in Lecco. That is where she met her husband-to-be. He was selling machinery for the factory in which she was a receptionist. My mother was very pretty and in love with American cinema."

Maddie closed the book and hugged it to herself. "My mother never wrote me a letter until Nonna Ida died." She looked at Gracie, her clipped tone betrayed by her obvious pent-up longing. "No, we are not close. Perhaps we never can be."

Gracie wanted to pull Maddie into her arms. Instead, she said, "You came to the Midwest, within driving distance of Cleveland." She searched the girl's eyes, probing deeply. "Surely, you came here for a reason?"

"Curiosity," Maddie said in a deceptively quiet voice. "But I am a safe distance from her."

This time, Gracie went with the urge and reached for Maddie, who leaned in to meet her. *Oh, Lord, how can I help this child?*

Uncle Miltie was reading the instructions to the new garage-door opener when Gracie arrived home. Rocky hovered over him, impatient to get the project started.

"You don't have to count every washer and screw," the editor told him. "Come on, man."

Uncle Miltie wagged a finger. "A job worth doing is a job worth doing right! We are not going to rush into anything."

"Hello, boys!" she called, entering the fray. She eyed her uncle, who had refused to purchase the very same new opener when she'd offered to buy one just the other day.

"It was on sale," he said sheepishly.

Rocky exhaled frustration. "The man won't listen to reason. He wouldn't buy the model with the better remote control, and now he thinks we have to inventory the incidentals before we get started." And to Uncle Miltie: "I say we do it, worry about what's missing later. Sure we inventory the big parts, but if we're missing a screw or something like that, we improvise. We've got one of these gizmos in a thousand pieces, surely something from the old one will fit anything we could possibly be missing!"

"I told the man I could handle the job myself," her uncle said, scowling. "He thinks you're going to feed him, and that's the only reason he came along. Send him home, Gracie!" More mock-angry than seriously so, Uncle Miltie still wasn't entirely teasing,

She put her hands on her hips, eyeing one and then the other. "You fight nice, boys! I'll get our meal around." She looked at her friend. "And, Rocky, you *are* staying for supper."

She hadn't even reached the kitchen when Sophie called just to let her know that Abe seemed in good spirits. Gracie impulsively invited the brother and sister to join them for dinner.

She then scoured the cupboards to find an acceptable arrangement of ingredients. A tuna noodle casserole seemed fine. She would dress it up with a tossed salad and crusty, hot bread. Retrieving a frozen loaf of her last homemade batch, she set about fixing the meal. Some of her three-bean salad would make a quick piquant side dish to contrast with the creaminess of the casserole. She would do a deep-dish cherry cobbler for dessert. Rocky had a soft spot for cherries. And for cobblers, too.

When everyone had gathered, Gracie lit the candles on the table, their warm glow making her simple fare seem like a gourmet meal.

"Lovely," Abe said, taking his seat beside her. "Do I detect a hint of tarragon?"

Gracie laughed. "You do." And to Sophie. "My tuna noodle casserole is a hurry-up recipe using canned soup, but it doesn't mean I can't season it with my imagination. Your brother has a sharp nose."

"My *mind* may be going," Abe said, glancing at his sister. "But the sniffer is still top-notch."

Gracie concluded that their disagreement still had not been resolved, so she steered the conversation in a different direction. "I spent a lovely afternoon in the library with Maddie."

"She's a treasure," Abe said. "I told her I would adopt her any day. But then how would I explain to my Amy?"

"I *hope* you meant it, actually," Sophie said. "Maddie has approached me about switching host families. She thinks she and Amy would get along better if they lived apart."

Sophie looked at her brother. "I was going to wait to tell you, but we are among friends. And Amy already mentioned it to Gracie. Maddie wants to finish the year with us."

Abe's attention was on his sister. "What is this *us*? You are going back to Cleveland!"

"I don't have to." Sophie scanned the group, perhaps trying to garner support. "I can stay as long as you like."

Abe brushed her offer away with a wave of his hand. "I'm doing all right by myself. You can go home anytime."

"You're *not* doing all right!" She pleaded with him, "You need me!"

Gracie looked at Rocky, who shrugged his shoulders. She searched her mind for something to distract them, but it was Uncle Miltie who changed the direction of the conversation. "You know, I was built backwards."

Attention turned to him, so he leaned back in his chair, milking it for all it was worth.

"Yeah?" Rocky said. "So, tell us something we didn't know."

Gracie humored her uncle. "I know there's a punch line."

"My nose runs and my feet smell." He looked at them expectantly, his eyes twinkling. Then he led them in the laughter they couldn't deny him.

After that, they slipped into small talk, and Rocky updated them on some upcoming community events he'd gleaned from his paper's calendar pages. Uncle Miltie shared some of the happenings at the senior center where he volunteered, saying the kids at the daycare center were hosting a Grandparents' Day for all the surrogates they'd come to love, and that he was going to be master of ceremonies for the event.

As Gracie served the dessert, the conversation turned to Maddie and the upcoming International Fair at the church. Gracie updated them on Barb's plans and progress.

Amy and her mother had taken charge of the banquet and were lining up folks willing to cook or provide a donation for the ingredients. Several of the exchange students had agreed not only to provide a favorite recipe, but also to help with preparation.

"Sounds wonderful," Sophie said, and looking at her brother, "I'm thinking we could do one of the recipes from our mother—something authentically Jewish."

"We would love it!" Gracie was sure she spoke for everyone in the congregation. "Over the years, with all discussions, Abe and I have discovered that Christianity and Judaism are connected in more ways than you might imagine!"

Rocky was not to be outdone. "The newspaper, of course, will interview some of the foreign students. That way, people will know something ahead of time about some of the students they'll meet."

"Maddie can give you their names," Sophie told him. "I'll talk to her about it at work tomorrow. Amy's been so busy that we've been using her more often."

Gracie decided not to introduce the issue of Amy's feeling pushed out. She would do her best to make sure the girl felt included—but right now *esprit de corps* seemed most important.

"I forgot to mention, I have an appointment with Gordon Welty on Monday," Sophie told Abe. "He called from Cleveland before we came here tonight. He talked to my broker about freeing up some of my funds."

"You going to invite me, or inform me afterward that you've sold my business out from under me?"

Sophie folded her hands on the table, and waited. Her expression clearly indicated that her brother had insulted her. Abe concentrated on his salad. After a tense moment, she continued, "We are going to talk about investments—in general. Gordon was a stockbroker long before he ventured into the food industry and started recruiting investors of his own. He has some leads for me to explore. He's not sure my broker is doing the best he can with my money."

She looked to Gracie. "I have a little capital I want to grow. We have got to do what we can. Social Security is not going to take care of us. I know you don't trust Welty, but he *is* a good businessman. And he knows the market."

"He doesn't know *me*," Abe said, exercising his cantankerousness.

Sophie smiled demurely at her brother. "At this point in my life, I need to be very careful with my investments. Don't worry, dear brother, I am not going to do anything impulsive. And I wouldn't dream of trying to go behind your back and sell your precious deli. How could I, even if I wanted to?"

She looked at Gracie. "Welty told me that his project may

not be well received in Willow Bend. I think he mentioned talking to you about this." And to her brother. "So you see, he is not trying to *steal* your business. He may just choose another town."

"I don't trust the man," Uncle Miltie said.

Rocky laced his fingers. "Everyone at this table qualifies for senior citizen discounts. We've all put in sixty-plus decades of life, and I'm feeling your discomfort in what is really going on here. We hate the idea of Abe having any problems, because the same ones may soon be ones we're facing."

He made a point of making eye contact with each one of them. "Today it is Abe. Tomorrow us. What do we want from life? What do we expect from our children and the next generation? Do they owe us anything? Do we owe them? We each have to decide. I guess that will determine where we hold our ground."

"For me it is in my deli," Abe said. "This place has been my life for thirty-five years. I am not willing to let go of it just yet.

"Maybe my mind *is* going, I'm not sure. What I am certain of is that I am *alive*. And as long as I am alive, I am going to *live*! For me, that means opening up my restaurant every morning, and greeting my customers with that corny line about the special being two dollars and ninety-five cents and advice free."

His expression softened as he faced his sister. "I love you,

Sophie. I want my friends to hear me tell you that. I love you with all my heart. I can't put into words how much your support has meant to me. But, sister dear, I am my own man. This is *my* business. I will make my own decisions. Please, give me the same respect you would give your friends."

Gracie wanted to applaud, but the hurt in Sophie's eyes hit close to home. She loved her family and wanted the best for them, too. Her heart went out to both brother and sister.

"You know," Rocky began, "when I began to qualify for senior citizen discounts, at first I was taken aback, thinking I was too young. Then I liked the idea of being treated in a special way by virtue of my age. Businesses were giving me more respect than my young colleagues. But then I realized those businesses just wanted my money!"

He sighed. "Money. That's the bottom line. Productivity is measured by material success. Does anybody look at what Uncle Miltie does at the seniors center? How do we put a price tag on the service those seniors give the little ones in the daycare center? When is the market value of thirty-something years of hard work best cashed in? Money again." He scanned the group. "We've grown beyond that. We know money can't buy anything that is important to us. So, why do we let ourselves be seduced by it?"

Gracie wanted to kiss the man.

AFTER SEVERAL DAYS OF RAIN, on the first dry morning Gracie was anxious to get back to prayer-walking. She donned her earphones and cassette player, and prepared to set out. Gooseberry, equally ready for exercise, was at her heels. She bent to stroke him, and he rubbed against her legs, purring.

"Sometimes I wish people were a little more like cats," Gracie told Uncle Miltie. "You always know where you stand with them. No pretenses."

Uncle Miltie nodded. "I'll give you that. But I'll take a dog any day." He peered at Gooseberry. "You hear that? D-O-G."

Gracie scooped her cat into her arms, and after giving him some attention allowed him to jump to the floor. "You need anything?"

"A new body." Uncle Miltie rubbed his hip. "This one is giving me fits. It's not aging that gets you, it's the ailments. A couple of rainy days, and I'm ready to pack it in."

Her uncle hated medicine and only took what was absolutely necessary, so she needed nearly to force him to take the occasional arthritis-strength aspirin for his aches.

"You are doing great, getting back on your feet. Why, it seems only yesterday you were dependent on that walker! Now, you can do almost anything with the help of your cane. You ought to be proud of all the progress you've made!"

"What choice did I have?" He grimaced, adjusting his weight to accommodate an apparent pain in the lower back. "I couldn't die." He chuckled. "Couldn't even roll over! Roll over and die, get it?"

"Say," he began, "that reminds me of a good one I heard at the center.

"An old man was wondering if his wife had a hearing problem, see. So one night, he stands behind her while she's cooking. He whispers, 'Honey, can you hear me?' No response, so he moves a little closer and says again, 'Honey, can you hear me?' Still no response. Finally he moves right behind her and says, 'Honey, can you hear me?' She says loudly, 'For the third time, *Yes!*'"

Gracie laughed and hugged him, which pleased her uncle immensely.

"I won't be home this afternoon. By the time I get back from my walk, you'll already be gone to read to the kids. I've got some errands to catch up on, and then I'm going to stop at the Cantrells'. I got out that big book on Mason County, and I think Maddie would enjoy looking it over. And some-time today, I want to pop in the deli and check on Abe."

"Oh, I forgot to mention that Estelle called when you were in the bathroom this morning." He smiled teasingly. "She's walking your route, and hopes to meet up with you along the way. She mentioned something about the *two* of you stop-ping at the deli."

"Actually, Uncle Miltie, Estelle is a really nice woman underneath all her pretensions. I'm sure of it."

"Nice, if you like piranhas!" he harrumphed. "That woman will eat you alive!"

She shot him a warning glance, the very look of disap-proval that could make both El and Arlen squirm. "No mat-ter how crusty a person is—"

"I know, I know. There's always some cream filling inside." He ambled toward the half-full thermos. "You get going. I'm just going to have a cup of coffee before Les picks me up."

Gracie was grateful for Lester Twomley. He was not only a fine tenor, but, like Rocky, was a good friend to her uncle. Les was pretty handy with wood, to boot, and had rigged up a special step so Uncle Miltie could get into his small pickup truck. "Tell him I think he's doing a great job with the music Barb's chosen."

He nodded, waving her off before reaching into the cookie jar.

Gracie and Gooseberry had just rounded the first corner on

their walk when they met Estelle coming in the opposite direction. She had a matching cassette player and headphones.

"Good morning, Estelle!"

The woman slipped off her headphones and pushed the
Off button on the player. "I opted for a book-on-tape. I love
a good romance, and now they have these inspirational ones!
They give me a lift."

This was another surprise. "I like mysteries, myself," she
admitted, "but I, too, have a soft spot for a good love story."

"And I don't mind a good mystery, when it comes to it."

Gooseberry, unstimulated by the literary turn of the conversation, turned back in the direction of home. After a
minute or so Gracie heard the squawking of catbirds. They'd
discovered the whereabouts of their archenemy. Gracie
turned to see her alarmed pet ducking into the bushes just a
whisker ahead of the retaliation-minded birds.

When she determined he'd safely escaped that sortie, she
put her attention back on Estelle, who was saying "Speaking
of mysteries, I heard Welty was snooping down in the base-
ment at the courthouse. A friend of mine—you know Avis
Murphy—works in the office there and says that he's been
checking old deeds."

"I thought he'd gone back to Cleveland." Gracie remembered him saying that when she'd talked to him. "When did
Avis see him? Maybe I misheard him."

Estelle rubbed her chin. "I thought it was yesterday. Yes, it was yesterday. That's when I saw Avis. She was going to lunch just as I was coming in. Welty passed us going out. I said something like, 'I wonder what he's doing here' and she told me that he'd been in there several times. They were all a little curious about him."

Gracie wondered why Welty had lied to her. Of course, he could have changed his plans. Now, though, she wished Ann O'Neill had been free to share more. Representing Welty meant she was bound by attorney-client privilege. Gracie made a note to talk to Rocky, but for now Estelle seemed interested, and thus not a bad person with whom to share her suspicions. Gracie updated her on what they'd learned of his dealings in Willow Bend.

"Do you think Welty could have anything to do with Abe's accidents?" Estelle's question surprised her, for Gracie had begun to wonder exactly that.

"I've hated to entertain that thought, even for an instant," Gracie confessed, "but, still, there's been a nagging suspicion. I've been afraid to voice it, because it sounds so awful."

Estelle agreed. "It crossed my mind several times when I heard Welty's name mentioned in connection with Abe's accidents. But if he's checking on deeds . . . I don't know what to think. Oh yes, and he's been doing some research on old wills as well."

"Does your friend know what property or whose will?" Gracie asked.

Estelle shook her head. "I asked Ruth. She said folks are curious. He's pretty conspicuous in a small courthouse like ours, but nobody out and out snoops. She wondered if I knew anything about him."

Gracie wanted to talk to Rocky, for he always seemed to have a way of getting information to which she didn't have access. Perhaps it was time he did some investigating on a certain entrepreneur from Cleveland.

Abe was in good spirits when they arrived at the deli. He and his sister had worked on their differences, and she had decided to try to give him some space, departing early that morning for Cleveland. She was going to start putting the sale of her house into motion, and visit her broker.

"So what will you have?" Abe pulled the menu from behind the napkin dispenser. "The special is still special." He smiled. "Advice is still free."

Gracie put her hand to the menu. "Just a glass of pineapple juice for me."

"I'll take a bagel with cream cheese," Estelle said. "That is, if they're fresh."

"What do you mean *fresh*!" Abe feigned indignation. "I make them every morning." They all laughed.

"Are the girls going to come in after school?" Gracie asked.

"Amy is. I don't need both of them."

"So what did you decide about Maddie moving in with you?"

"Sophie called her last night after we had our little talk." He sought Gracie's gaze. "I love my sister, but we can't live together. We both realize it. I agreed to have medical tests, and if there is something . . . well, we'll cross that bridge when we come to it.

"I would be happy to house the girl," he went on, "but I'm a single man. Okay, and I'm an *old* bachelor. Probably not a host the exchange organization would approve."

"I'm going to stop by to see the Cantrells after school," Gracie told them. "Thought I'd talk to Linda. Hopefully, we can figure out a way to help the girls get along better."

"I think I understand how Amy feels," Estelle interjected. "Maddie is getting a lot of attention. Everyone likes her, and it's so hard for Amy to make friends in the first place. Perhaps Amy is feeling a bit . . . overlooked."

Gracie hadn't thought of Estelle in this light. The woman always overtly craved the limelight, while offering her opinions on almost every subject.

Abe reflected for a moment. "I would never want the child to think I don't appreciate her. Why, Amy is indispensable, like I said, she reads me like a book." He looked at Gracie. "But I like Maddie, too. She'll listen to my stories."

"That's my point!" Estelle said, "Even *this* place used to be

Amy's turf! Maddie has usurped her position almost every-where. I've noticed it at church. Everyone talks to Maddie, she's a novelty. And, of course, she has that cute accent."

Gracie nodded, appreciating her friend's acumen and wondering why she seemed for a change more thoughtful than bossy.

Linda Cantrell was cutting vegetables for soup when Gracie arrived with a book for Maddie, who had gone out with her area representative. Gracie put the gift on the counter, offering to help.

She wielded a knife and chopped celery. The aroma of beef stock and herbs pleasantly filled the air. A cozy kitchen *was* also the best place for friends to solve problems.

"Amy has always been sensitive," Linda explained. "And I hate to admit it, but my daughter often misses the silver lining because she only sees the storm cloud on the horizon. She's a lot like my husband. I love them both for their prac-ticality, but they both can be very singleminded, not willing to see another side to a situation. I try to encourage Amy not to take everything so seriously, but it's simply her nature."

Linda lifted the lid on the pot. "It's ready for the vegetables."

Gracie pushed the mixture of carrots and celery into the steamy broth. "I'm often guilty of the same thing."

"Me, too." Linda smiled. "But combined with teenage hormones and impulsiveness, it's often volatile!"

Gracie and Arlen had weathered enough of those storms for her to appreciate Linda's position. "Thank goodness they do outgrow it," she told her friend.

"That's what I tell myself." Linda sighed. "Roy says someday she'll call me blessed, but for now . . . I guess we just survive."

Linda put the lid on the pan. "You probably know, Sophie can't take Maddie."

"Abe told me today."

"Maddie told us right after Sophie called. Although she and Amy have been getting along a little better, Maddie— who misses her grandmother—really appreciates Sophie and did hope to stay with them."

Gracie took a whiff of the soup. "Basil . . . parsley . . . *nutmeg*?"

Linda nodded. "I'm not the chef you are, but I love to cook. I am always delighted to hear that you are catering an event, Gracie. I know how delicious everything will be."

Gracie accepted the compliment, but was more interested in helping the girls. "So, what will happen now that Sophie and Abe can't take Maddie?"

"She'll stay with us. Like I said, we've grown very fond of her. Even Amy. Don't worry, we'll be fine. And International Night seems just the thing to draw them closer. Amy is a detail person, and I've seen them discussing plans. I think helping organize it together will be good for both of them."

Linda paused. "You've been the best possible friend. I don't know what I can say to tell you how much I appreciate your concern for Amy and our family."

"One family in the Lord," she reminded Linda. Gracie extended a hand to the other woman's shoulder. "We're all in this together. Children belong to all of us."

"Okay," Linda said, "then I'm going to tell you the truth." She paused, seeming to weigh her words. "Maddie was not happy after the telephone call from Sophie. You might even say she was downright hostile. She slammed every door between the kitchen telephone and her bedroom. She told Roy she was ready to go home to Italy. I *would* appreciate your talking to her, Gracie. Tell her we care about her. We want her to stay. Amy does, too."

Linda glanced at the book on the counter. "I wish I had been the one to think to do that. I get so busy, it's easy to overlook opportunities to demonstrate love. She told me about meeting you in the library. She was very touched to discover you reading about Italy. I haven't done as much."

"You've opened your home." Gracie smiled. "You're making homemade soup. In Uncle Miltie's book, you're a saint!"

Linda let herself laugh.

"When will Maddie be home?"

"About six. The area rep took her to Jamie's Dairy for a soda to talk about the situation."

Gracie took the book with her, promising to return the next day when she could spend some time with Maddie.

The following afternoon, Gracie received a hysterical call from Sophie, who was en route from Cleveland to Willow Bend. Abe was in the hospital—he'd apparently overdosed on his medication.

Gracie calmed her friend, telling her she would head over to Keefer Memorial immediately. She called Rocky, who swung by to pick her up. Gracie had promised to stay with Abe until Sophie arrived, but she found the Cantrell family in the waiting lounge when she arrived at the emergency room. Maddie was with them.

Roy stood to greet her. "Amy found him. He was sitting at his desk in the kitchen of the deli, apparently going over invoices. At first, she thought he'd just fallen asleep. When he didn't respond to shaking, she called me. I told her to call 911. He was groggy but awake by the time they arrived. Maddie found the bottle of pills, sitting by his cup of tea. He couldn't remember taking more than his prescribed dose."

Linda joined them. "They want to eliminate the possibility that it was a mild heart attack or stroke, so they're running a few tests."

"It was probably the pills." Roy reasoned, "It could happen to anyone."

His wife fidgeted, as if struggling to accept what could only seem obvious. Did she also suspect Abe was experiencing diminished capacity? Gracie glanced at Rocky, who was frowning in concentration.

Linda gave a quick side glance to Maddie, who sat quietly in a chair in the corner, her hands folded in her lap. Did Linda hesitate for just the flick of an eyelash?

"Maddie remembers him taking his medication when she brought the tea. Abe claims he took it hours earlier. We were so worried, we came right to the hospital. Thank God he's all right!"

"Why don't we do just that," Gracie suggested, reaching for Linda's hand to pray.

Linda startled. "Pray? Here? Now?"

Amy rose to join them. "It's the best we can do. Thank you for reminding us, Gracie."

Maddie stood quietly behind her friend.

Opening her heart to the Lord was the most natural thing. Gracie was frightened for Abe, and told God as much. *He's always been a strong man,* she reminded God. *But strong men need You every bit as much as the weaker ones, sometimes even more. I pray for Abe as I would my dearest family member. He is a brother of the spirit to me.*

She had just said "Amen" when the doctor appeared.

"His EKG is normal. Neurological fine. No muscle

problems, pupils equal and reactive. I think he'll be just fine," the doctor confirmed.

"Can we take him home?" Linda wanted to know.

"He's a little disoriented, but I don't see why he can't go if someone is going to stay with him until his sister gets back."

"I will," Gracie and Linda said in unison.

Rocky was the tie-breaker. "*I'll* stay with him. He'd probably feel more comfortable with an insensitive lug like me, than with either half of a pair of mother hens fussing over him. He'll get that from Sophie. Besides, Abe owes me a chess rematch when he's up to it. One of you can spell me for a while later on."

Gracie noticed when they gathered around Abe in the hospital lobby that both Amy and Maddie stayed in the background. Neither girl said anything to the other.

Abe was groggy, but in good spirits, apologizing for his apparent stupidity. He was enough himself to resent being forced to depart the hospital in a wheelchair, protesting grumpily.

"I drank milk once with a prescription I shouldn't have," Roy tried to distract him. "Man, did I get sick!"

Linda nodded. "We've all probably made similar mistakes."

"It could happen to anyone," Rocky said.

Gracie sensed they were all wondering the same thing—could Abe's mind really be slipping?

Rocky dropped by Gracie's place later that evening, having allowed Linda to relieve him. Gracie fixed them both a cup of tea, as Uncle Miltie quizzed him on the evening's events. Sophie was due in the next day.

"Peculiar thing is that Abe really doesn't recall taking the second dose. Last thing he remembers is sitting down to write bills. He felt logy, but not sick. The next thing he knew, he was stretched out on a gurney."

Uncle Miltie stirred a second teaspoon of sugar into his tea. "It's not so peculiar. I had a stomach relaxant that could put me in la-la land in five minutes flat. Thank goodness, I never double-dipped that medication!"

"Anithistamines sometimes knock me silly," Gracie admitted, "but Abe wasn't just groggy. He was out cold."

Rocky nodded. "Dr. Hawley, the guy who was on duty, said it was a strong reaction—not severe enough to keep him for extended observation, but enough to warrant concern."

"But he's all right." Gracie wanted reassurance.

"He's fine. Sophie has told the nurses she doesn't want Abe staying alone until they finish the battery of tests, so I guess she's coming back for another extended visit."

Rocky looked at Gracie over the edge of his cup, as though

testing the waters. "It appears to be the case that the first symptoms of dementia often go undetected, and many doctors are not trained to recognize the warning signs."

"Man, oh man." Uncle Miltie said. "Who would have thought it would hit Abe Wasserman?"

Gracie's rebuke was gentle. "Let's not jump to conclusions."

"It's looking like more than speculation," Rocky warned. "With his recent history of accidents, I'm inclined to agree with Sophie."

She silently agreed things did not look good, but Rocky's conclusion was too pat. There was more to it, she was sure of it.

Gracie ventured, "Estelle and I were talking about this recent series of accidents. We agreed that they seem too coincidental, too close together in time."

"What are you thinking, Gracie?" Rocky wanted to know.

It was time to put her cards on the table. "I'm wondering about Gordon Welty. Don't you think it strange that he was around during all the episodes? Abe's problems didn't start until he arrived in town."

The silence that followed was so absolute that Gracie could almost hear Gooseberry's whiskers twitch.

Old deeds. Wills. A Victorian mansion, and a fifties deli. What did they all have in common? Add to that a possible poisoning, and a mysterious investor from the big city, and they had a full-fledged mystery unfolding!

"So what are you suggesting, Gracie, my girl?" She had her uncle's interest piqued, anyway. "Welty is orchestrating this whole thing?"

"But the guy's in Cleveland," Rocky pointed out.

Gracie gave a little shiver as she corrected him, "No he's not!"

THE NEXT MORNING dawned picture-perfect, so Gracie decided she'd walk over to visit Abe at his home. But after calling the Wassermans, she discovered her quarry was back at work! Sophie had arrived to find him heading to the deli. Apparently, he was taking out his frustration with himself by kneading bread dough.

Gracie was almost to the deli when she heard squawking. Catbirds!

"Gooseberry!"

Her pet had been trailing her, using the hedges and shrubbery for camouflage from his feathered stalkers. She stooped to scold him, but those liquid gold eyes melted her anger. She couldn't very well return him to her house, not now that she was so close.

"Well, let's hope Abe doesn't mind visitors of the feline

variety," Gracie told her cat, afraid of letting him roam in Willow Bend's inconsequential, but busy, commercial district. There wasn't much to distinguish it from the surrounding neighborhoods, but Main Street led out of town, and many folks traveled that way to jobs in the surrounding area. It was not the place for a much-loved cat to be wandering. Even if the whole town knew him.

She scooped Gooseberry up in her arms and opened the door to the deli. "Cats allowed?" she called, thrusting the tabby front and center.

"Gracie!" Abe stepped out from behind the counter. "Who is that you have there, Gooseberry?"

"He followed me, do you mind if he comes in?"

Abe chuckled. "Not at all! Here—wait a sec and I'll have a dish of milk to tempt him. Like my advice, it's free!"

She followed him to the counter. "I just wanted see you, make sure for myself that you're okay."

"Well, come on back in the kitchen. I'll put you to work. I've got bread cooling, just about ready to bag."

Gracie drew in a deep breath of yeast-scented air. "Smells delicious! Suppose we cut a loaf?"

"Challah, all right? I was going to take this home tonight. Sophie can't eat a whole loaf. I'll toast you a slice."

Gooseberry snooped, poking his nose in all the corners, perhaps hoping for a mouse hole. Gracie wasn't ready to share her suspicions about Welty and the accidents, but she decided to ask Abe why he thought the man might be searching deeds and checking wills.

"It must involve the Carruthers place," he said. "Because I bought this place free and clear. Saved for years, and with a little bit of help from my grandfather's estate, paid cash. Bought it from Ernie Taggart, who inherited it from his father. No, Welty's going to come up empty if that's where he's searching."

Rocky called her later that afternoon. "I ran a check on Welty. It seems the man has a history of speculative investing. I also talked to a detective friend of mine in Cleveland. Welty's lost a lot of dough in more than one venture. Lucky for him, there's always been a widow or two in the wings to bail him out, so he's always landed on his feet. Let's hope Sophie isn't his latest patsy!"

"Then it *has* to be him behind Abe's accidents," she reasoned. "You know as well I do that Abe can't be going senile."

Rocky's reply was measured. "Gracie, you know I trust your judgment in most things, but this is a medical matter where neither of us have the proper expertise."

"Seriously, don't you think Welty is behind this?"

It was quiet on the other end for a long minute.

"Fraud, embezzling money from lonely old women, even

manipulating court documents, seems reasonable. But putting a guy's keys in the freezer? Come on Gracie, that's a long stretch."

She filled a cup with water and stuck it the microwave. "I just have this uncanny feeling that something isn't right. All these accidents in a matter of days."

"There may be many more that have gone unnoticed. I don't honestly think Abe would even tell us if there were others. It may just be timing. I mean, Sophie is here again, to see what is going on. For sure, this time. You can bet she'll be watching!"

The timer went off, and Gracie fixed a cup of tea for herself. "Maybe I should speak to the girls, see if they noticed anything prior to Welty's arrival."

"I'm going to stay with the real estate angle. You can warn Sophie, tell her she's involved with someone who may be up to no good." Another pause. "Gracie, just don't mention your suspicions about the accidents, okay? No need to get her—or Abe—upset."

She felt a twinge of indignation. "I wasn't going to!"

When Rocky hung up, she decided to put her trust in her own intuition, despite her friend's skepticism. *Lord*, she said, *I do feel You guide my thoughts to solutions I can't see on my own. You know my love for Abe and concern for him are never enough to make me want to suspect someone falsely of wrongdoing. Help me, as You always do, to see the truth.*

Gracie phoned Sophie at the deli. She was just on her way home. Gracie suggested she stop by for tea. When she arrived, she had Maddie with her, having run into her on Main Street. "I can't stay long," Sophie reminded her. "Abe's closing up and I want to be there when he gets to the house."

Gracie decided against telling Sophie about Welty in the presence of Maddie, so they made small talk. One subject that came up was International Night. Maddie and Amy had put up posters and made sure an open invitation was in the Sunday bulletin. It looked to be a grand event. Gracie voiced her hope that a big support crew had been enlisted. Maddie was confident that Amy and her mother had that angle covered, as well.

"Tea does restore one so." Sophie took another sip.

"It goes to the spirit as well as the stomach," Gracie agreed.

"My grandmother made her own teas. She had one for whatever ails you. I told Signor Abe, she even had brews to improve your memory and to relieve your worry. I was sad he didn't seem interested."

Gooseberry nudged between her legs and Maddie bent to rub his head. But the cat was more interested in her macramé purse. Gracie apologized, but Maddie was amused at his feline antics. "I never have had a pet."

"I don't think I could live without one," Gracie said. "Especially not this old guy. He's been with me a long time."

Sophie smiled. "I used to have a dog. A good friend. He died a year or so back and I didn't have the heart to replace him."

Gooseberry batted at the strings, and nudged his face against the handbag. Then, still lying on the floor, he pulled it in toward him with his front paws. Maddie giggled with delight.

Gracie watched him for a minute. "He acts almost as goofy when he roots in the catnip I plant for him in my garden!"

Maddie picked up her purse and put it on her lap before gently stroking the belly of the cat, who had rolled over. He certainly was content.

Gracie hated jumping to conclusions, and she was impatiently waiting for Rocky to come through with more information on Welty and his business at the courthouse. She could not bring herself to find some pretext to snoop through the records. What if the man might actually be on the up-and-up?

It was Carol Whitefield who unexpectedly provided another piece to the puzzle. It was at the Historical Society's bi-monthly meeting. During the coffee hour, Gracie discovered from the real estate agent that Gordon Welty was indeed interested in the Carruthers mansion—*and* the deli as well. Perhaps Rocky was right, and the former was the intended parking lot.

"He's seems pretty confident that he can snag both properties," Carol confided. "He's discovered a loophole somewhere in one of the deeds, I think. I wonder if I should make sure someone gives Abe a tip as to what's going on...."

Cordelia Fountain's lips were pinched. "He acted like he cared about historical places! I talked to him myself!"

All Gracie could think about was her friend and his several simultaneous dilemmas. What was Abe going to do if he somehow had mistaken his ownership of the property that housed not only his livelihood but his very soul?

Just at that moment, as Gracie was experiencing twinges of helpless despair—so upset was she on her friend's behalf—the very object of her fear appeared on the raised podium at the end of the room. Gordon Welty was following Eleanor McIver, the Society's current president, who rapped for the gathering's attention.

"Well, well, well," Carol said, softly. "Perhaps he's finally going to let the cat out of the bag."

11

APPARENTLY THE CAT would remain in the bag!

Eleanor introduced Gordon Welty as a fellow genealogy buff and informed her listeners that he was making a generous donation to their contingency fund. The room politely applauded, and then the rest of the business of the meeting was taken up.

It was Marge who approached him afterwards, curiosity unchecked. When it came to Willow Bend's newest benefactor, Gracie for the time being preferred to stay in the background.

"Well, well, well, it seems you are serious about settling here. You gave us the impression that it was still tentative." Marge extended her hand. "Welcome to our town. Will you be relocating here soon?"

"I am staying at Mrs. Fountain's. It meets my needs for

now. I travel between Chicago and Cleveland quite often, and this is a good halfway point."

Marge tried again. "Perhaps you'll remodel the old Carruthers place, and live in it yourself. The preservation-minded among us would be so pleased."

He made a non-committal shrug. "We'll see. Now, if you'll excuse me, Cordelia wants me to meet the others on the committee." To Gracie: "It's nice to see you again, Mrs. Parks."

She returned his greeting, and braved, "I thought you were going back to Cleveland for a few days."

"Plans change. Cordelia invited me to your society's lunch, so I felt it would be wise to stay. You're right, Mrs. Parks, everyone in Willow Bend does seem to know everyone else's business. But Cordelia is not just my host, she's a fascinating local historian."

Marge and Gracie just had time to raise their eyebrows at one another before he disappeared out the door.

"Gracie, did you get a chance to talk to Sophie?" Rocky suddenly was in front of her, having exchanged greetings with some of the departing members. "I knew I'd find you here."

"No, not yet. She had Maddie with her, and I didn't think it was good timing."

"Well, you better talk to her," he told her. "Abe saw his lawyer this morning. I dropped in for a sandwich and he told me he's given Sophie power-of-attorney."

Gracie looked at him, perplexed. "Arlen has my power-of-attorney. It's just good sense."

"Unless somebody is convinced you're already not capable of making decisions."

He wasn't usually alarmist. She knew it was his affection for their friend that was making him so. "She and Welty are close. And, as we've all observed, the man is slick. He could convince Sophie it might be time to exercise that power."

Providentially, Gracie ran into Sophie at the Willow Mart. Some people call it coincidence, but Gracie knew otherwise. *Everything happens for a reason, dear Lord,* she affirmed. *I know that. You keep life mysterious, it's true, but that never seems to stop me from trying to figure it out!*

"Gracie, I appreciate the extra pair of arms," Sophie exclaimed, as they carried her purchases, several bags worth, to Abe's car.

"Sophie, I need to talk to you . . . . if you have a few moments now, we could get some ice cream. Indulge ourselves." Then, thinking of the bags she'd just helped carry, she added, "Unless you've got something that will melt."

"It's all cleaning supplies." Sophie told her. "A clean house and a clean heart guarantees a happy life, my mother used to say. Abe has a regular cleaning woman, but it needs a thorough going-over—to my mind, anyway. I think it'll cheer him up, too."

"Well, I just have a few non-perishables. So what do you say we meet at The Sweet Shoppe?"

"Do they serve butterscotch sundaes?"

Gracie grinned. "That—and more. All with cherries on top, and two if you beg."

"You're on!"

Over coffee and sundaes, Gracie unfolded their discoveries about Gordon Welty, keeping her suspicion about Abe's memory incidents to herself.

"He really seems so sincere." Sophie shook her head. "Hazel Grossman introduced me to him. She raved about him, saying that he'd been the most wonderful advisor. She trusted him enough to invest in his first restaurant—that's been over a year ago. I just can't believe he's anything but honest."

Gracie decided to be frank. "He's left a trail of some dubious investments. It would worry *me*, even though I know nothing anyone ever invests in is a sure thing."

"I don't know what to think."

Gracie patted Sophie's hand. "Just be careful."

"He acts genuinely concerned about Abe." Sophie paused, eyes widening for a split second. "No, he wouldn't do that," she said, half-swallowing her words. Gracie could practically see the light bulb click on above her head.

"What is it?" She could only hope Sophie would soon arrive at the same conclusions she had herself.

Sophie shook her head, still not willing to share her dawning, even panicky, concern. She toyed nervously with the ring on her right hand, and looked past Gracie out the window. She sighed heavily, then sighed again.

And again.

After a long moment, she turned her head, searching out Gracie's gaze. A sardonic expression deepened the lines around Sophie's mouth and the fine wrinkles at the corners of her eyes. "I've always believed myself to be a keen judge of character, but if what you are telling me is true, then perhaps I have let myself be played for a fool.

"You see, it was Welty pressuring me to secure power-of-attorney for Abe. He felt that my brother's condition was deteriorating rapidly. He's even given me articles and pamphlets on dementia and Alzheimer's. I took it as just being helpful, passing on information so I'd know better what we were facing."

She sighed deeply again. "He's been telling me that his loyalty to Hazel, and the other women in our investment group, has been his only motivation for offering such a generous price for the deli. According to him, we're all in this venture together."

Sophie looked as if she might cry. "But who's to say what's really happening? Have I any guarantee that he has at heart my interests and those of the people who matter most to me?"

"Oh, Sophie!" Gracie confessed, "Similar thoughts have crossed my mind."

Her friend's violet eyes grew shrewd. "Well, he under-estimated his prey *this* time! Maybe I'll turn the tables and have a little surprise for Mr. Welty!"

She smiled conspiratorially. "Suppose I go along with him, play up my concern for Abe's health and my desire to move him to Florida with me."

"And see how he responds!" Gracie approved Sophie's strategy. "But what will you do? He hasn't really *done* anything illegal. There's still the possibility we could be wrong."

"Maybe even somehow he tricked my brother into taking that extra dose of medication." Sophie suddenly looked grave—and not a little frightened.

"But he wasn't in the deli that day!" said Gracie. "He may not even have been in town. He told me he was leaving for a few days, though a friend of Estelle's did see him in the courthouse the day after. Did he leave at all—for a day, or overnight? We still can't put him at the scene of the crime."

Sophie nodded, now pondering the fresh complications. "Did anyone talk to the girls about this? They were at the deli the day it happened."

"Why don't we talk to them together—you and I and the two of them. Maybe all of us together can produce some incriminating evidence."

It was Amy's afternoon to work, and Maddie seemed more than willing to join her at Sophie's request. Gracie was relieved to see them arrive joking with one another. Perhaps it was going to work out between them after all.

"You know, my dears, I'm worried about my brother's health, mentally and physically." Sophie looked to Gracie for support. "I'm trying to piece things together, and decide what I should do. What would be in his best interest."

Gracie nodded. "We were wondering about the accidental overdose."

Amy blanched, recalling the awful episode. *Perfectly normal response,* Gracie thought, *considering how it scared the girl.* It was Maddie's reaction that troubled her; she noticed a shadow pass over Maddie's guarded blue eyes.

Amy rattled off the details.

It had been after closing time. She'd just finished unloading the dishwasher, and then had gone in to tell Abe goodbye, when she discovered him slumped in his big wooden desk chair.

"Where was Maddie?" Sophie wanted to know.

Gracie glanced at Maddie, who sat quietly with her hands in her lap.

Sophie looked at the girl. "You said you fixed him tea."

"That was earlier," she said. Tripping over familiar words, as if flustered by Sophie's composure, Maddie told them that she had been in the deli after school with Amy, but then had a meeting with her area representative from the exchange program, and had left an hour or so before Amy closed up.

"Were there many customers?" Sophie asked.

Amy shook her head. "The regulars, picking up cold cuts or a loaf of bread for supper. We only served two or three at the counter. Mac Medline, and George from Miller's Feed, came in for coffee and sandwiches."

"Mr. Welty didn't stop by, did he?" Sophie asked.

Another negative.

"Amy, you said you found pills on the desk," Gracie remembered, "and that you took them with you to the hospital just in case. That was good thinking."

Amy dipped her gaze, blushing slightly. "It wasn't my idea, really. The paramedic told me to grab them."

"Did anyone check the bottle," Gracie asked Sophie, "to see how many were missing?"

Sophie held her palms out. "I thought of that, but Abe fills several prescriptions at a time, so he doesn't remember when he finished the last bottle. We couldn't tell."

Amy gave Maddie an odd glance. "Do they suspect it was something else?"

Sophie seemed to weigh her response. "We just want to be sure—for Abe's benefit." She looked at Gracie as if to ask, "What next?"

Suddenly an idea occurred to Gracie. "Did you fix him *herbal* tea?" she asked the Italian girl gently.

Tears welled, and Maddie bit her bottom lip. She sat without moving.

Sophie glanced between Gracie and the girl, obviously perplexed.

It was Amy who broke the silence. "It's time to tell them the truth, Maddie."

She moved to stand behind her friend, putting her hands around Maddie's shoulders. "She didn't mean to hurt him, really she didn't!"

"*What* is going on?" Sophie wanted to know.

Gracie guessed. "Maddie gave your brother some kind of herbal concoction, probably to make him sleep."

"*Si*." Maddie's voice was barely audible.

Amy looked at Gracie, her expression protective. "Her grandmother used it. Maddie told me it's supposed to improve your memory. It could help him, you know!"

Maddie lowered her head. "No, that's not true. I wanted him to fall asleep."

"What!" Sophie stared dumbstruck. Amy looked horrified. She removed her hands and stepped back.

Maddie burst into tears. "You were going home to Cleveland. I wanted you to stay. I miss my nonna.

"I knew the tea would not harm Signor Abe—it might even help! But I knew it would make him sleep if I brewed it extra strong—sleep more than an ordinary amount, I mean."

She lifted her head, tears streaming down her cheeks and

looked at Sophie. "It meant you would come back to him. I knew you would be afraid, and perhaps you would stay in Willow Bend. . . .

"I am so sorry!"

Sophie stared at the girl for a long moment, then pulled a linen handkerchief from her sleeve and wiped the girl's tears. "It still was a very unwise course of action, Maddie. You understand that, don't you?"

Maddie nodded.

"But I forgive you." Sophie's expression was kind. "It was insensitive of me not to recognize how attached you'd become."

She brushed wet strands of hair from Maddie's face. "I do care for you, perhaps more than I want to admit."

"Maddie's been obsessing over this," Amy said. "She's really sorry. I found her sitting in my closet crying, and coaxed her to tell me the truth." Amy looked to Gracie.

Maddie forced a smile. "Amy and I are more like sisters than we realized." She turned her attention to Sophie. "I was going to tell you, really I was."

And back to Gracie. "When Gooseberry played with my purse, I knew I had to tell the truth. I could not bear my conscience any longer. That is the day Amy found me in her closet."

"Ah, the herb you used affects cats!" Gracie smiled, realizing. "It was in your pocketbook!"

"You didn't do anything else, did you?" Gracie had to ask. "Like putting his keys in the freezer?"

Maddie blanched, then blushed red. "Oh, no! Never! I love Signor Abe. I would never do that." She lowered her gaze. "I did give him the strong tea, it is true. I knew you would think he took the medication twice." Then meeting Sophie's gaze again: "You have to believe me! I would never do that!"

Gracie and Sophie exchanged glances. That put them back at square one. Perhaps Abe was just aging, becoming more forgetful. But—that didn't explain Welty's actions. Unless he was cleverly opportunistic, determined to do whatever it took to convince Sophie to sell.

When Gracie got home, she called Rocky to fill him in on the turn of events. "There isn't anything the man can do without Sophie's consent, is there?"

"I wouldn't think so. But there's still more to this. Welty *has* filed what they call an Action To Quiet Title. He contends there is a some problem with the title—one that the owner can no longer resolve."

Gracie switched the walk-around receiver to the other ear so she could take notes. "What could it be?"

"Anything, really. An old lien, unpaid taxes. Thirty-five years ago, banks weren't so picky issuing mortgages. Now, with bankruptcy and lawsuits, they go over the deed with a fine-toothed comb."

Gracie underlined *Quiet Title*. "If it helps to know, Abe paid cash for the place. He told me as much."

"We'll know what's going on soon enough. Welty will either have to post in the newspaper his intention to buy a piece of property with an unclear title, or he'll start a civil action."

Her kitchen felt suddenly disquieting.

"He has seen a lawyer—Ann O'Neil."

She sensed Rocky shared her alarm. It was long moment until he said, "Maybe now's the moment for Abe to see one of his own."

Gracie shuddered as she hung up, not wanting to consider the possibilities. *Lord, I have to believe You knew what You were doing when You created lawyers. Certainly, as with the beasts and birds Noah gathered to shelter on the ark, they definitely come in pairs! At least, when one appears, another must always face him.*

Blinking, she was reminded how limited her vision really was, her mind fitting together only jigsaw pieces of the entire puzzle. *Lord, You see the whole unbroken picture. We need Your perspective on this.*

12

THE AFTERNOON BEFORE the International Dinner, Gracie greeted an enthusiastic ample kitchen crew. Maddie was there with a boy from the Czech Republic and two Germans. Marge had already snagged a Venezuelan girl to help her set the buffet table in readiness. Linda directed fellow choir members to peel potatoes and chop vegetables.

Gracie was looking forward to the evening as a diversion from her worries about Abe and what was really going on with Welty. Sophie had left several messages for him, which as far Gracie knew he had not returned. Cordelia Fountain assured them he was in town, although he frequently was gone for the whole day, not returning until late.

Her own main dish offering this evening was a hunter's stew, much like the cacciatore she had served Rocky. It seemed almost every country offered a similar recipe, and Willow Benders were plain folks, they enjoyed simple fair. How had Rocky described this dish? *Soulful.* Gracie liked that. She lifted the lid to the steamy dutch oven containing chicken with tomato sauce. "Smells delicious," she told Linda.

"We've got rice, as well as a nice boiled potato dish, for which Elke supplied a recipe. Josef, the boy from the Czech Republic is going to help Estelle make dumplings."

"What teamwork!" Gracie exclaimed. "And that's a professional opinion!"

"Amy and Maddie did a lot of the organizing," Linda explained. "You were right, Gracie. Planning this event was good for bringing them together."

She wondered whether Maddie had confessed her part yet in Abe's losing consciousness to Linda. Gracie silently prayed that Maddie would take care of that, if she hadn't already done so.

"We're expecting a hundred for dinner, more for the dessert bar." Linda beamed. "It was Amy's idea to offer the table of sampling sweets from many cultures."

Gracie knew that Sophie had made a large pot of *Shabbas* soup, thick with white beans and meat. But Abe would be supplying his famous cheesecake for the dessert table.

It had all the makings of a truly memorable night!

Just then, Rick Harding arrived, carrying a roasting pan. "A little taste of multi-cultural Americana—soul-fried chicken!" He put the pan on the counter and opened the oven. "Yep, room enough!"

He slid the pan in the oven. "I told Comfort we should whip up a batch of collard greens, but she wouldn't hear of it, saying one contribution was enough. Me, I could have cooked all day!"

The computer whiz was not only a great tenor, but also a terrific husband and father. His job allowed him a flexible schedule, so he could step into the role of Mr. Mom while his wife worked her hours as a nurse anesthesiologist. Gracie often appreciated his thoughts on navigating the rocky shoals of being a dual-career family—tips she'd tried to pass on gently to Arlen and Wendy.

"So how's your family?" Rick asked, slipping the mitt from his hand. "Your son and daughter-in-law get their childcare issues worked out?"

"They seem to have found a compromise," she told him, explaining Arlen's own job arrangement. "Wendy is really proud of him."

"Comfort is my biggest advocate, too." He leaned against the counter. "Folks are still leery of a man in the homemaker role, but she stands up for me. I think it's made our relationship stronger. We don't take each other's roles for granted anymore. We know from personal experience how hard both jobs are—care and homemaking."

And crossing his arms, he smiled, as though picturing his

petite wife with her warm eyes and smile that could light up a room. "I know I've come to appreciate Comfort even more here. She used to do all the housework herself, plus take care of the baby and manage a part-time career. We lived in the suburbs, and you'd be surprised how few stay-at-home moms there were. She felt outnumbered. And I didn't understand, insensitive oaf that I was."

Gracie laughed with him.

"A problem, I might add," he said, grinning, "I have not had since joining the ranks of part-time stay-at-home parents in Willow Bend. The mothers' group took me in as the poor, lost male. They think I don't have a clue about raising a four-year-old. It's been great!"

Rick canned their garden surplus, and could also knit better than most women she knew. Gracie had a feeling her friend could do anything else to which he set his mind, including outings in the park with the local mothers.

Maddie peeked around the corner. "I brought *tiramisú*." She handed the glass dish to Gracie. "It means 'pick-me-up.' Lots of sweet cream and mascarpone cheese flavored with coffee and chocolate. A favorite in my country."

"Did you make it?" Rick wanted to know.

That sweet smile. "Yes, with the help of my host mother."

Meanwhile, Gracie had taken the dessert from her and put it in the refrigerator.

Uncle Miltie appeared at the door with his military

scrapbook, obviously ready to declare victory over a captive audience. He lay the book on the only vacant counter and prepared to open it with much fanfare. To his chagrin, most of the kitchen crew were too busy to stop and listen, but Maddie and Rick gave him their attention.

"Thought you'd like to see the photographs of Italy," he told Maddie. "Of course, this is *long* before your time, but your grandmother would have been a young woman."

He chuckled. "I would have flirted with her, too, even if she was only half as pretty as you."

"*Zio* Miltie!" she scolded sweetly, with her Italian lilt.

Rick joined Maddie in examining the black-and-white snapshots, and Gracie moved behind them, positioning herself to see the pictures, too. Although Gracie had seen the album before, she always savored sharing his nostalgia. Linda joined her.

Maddie pointed to a photograph of a young man in uniform with dark hair and a dashing smile, flanked by two Italian soldiers. "This is you?"

Gracie craned her neck to see. It was a picture she didn't remember. She thought she'd seen them all, but then she hadn't known Uncle Miltie had served in Italy at the end of the war.

As her uncle gave the names of his two buddies, sharing their story of flushing a band of renegade Fascists out of the artillery-pocked farmhouse in the background, his features softened with a youthful glow. Then his expression turned pensive. Gracie had seen that look before. Uncle Miltie had spent time in a P.O.W. camp, and of that interval in his life he was uncharacteristically silent.

He apparently caught her stare, and pulled himself back to the present, returning to anecdotes from the period after the war ended. He described with obvious fondness the Italians, and his experiences with them.

Uncle Miltie hadn't seen those friends in more than fifty years, yet he spoke of them as if it had been only yesterday that they'd shared a victory cigar together in northern Italy.

"Guido here," Uncle Miltie said, pointing to a wiry man with what looked like a two-week stubble on his face, "hid out in the mountains when the Fascists came to conscript him. But as soon as the partisans advanced he joined them and fought to retake his town."

"My nonna's mother lived in a house like this one," Maddie told Uncle Miltie. "It had a secret passage to a field behind it, so the partisans could escape to the mountains without going through the village."

Rick was intrigued, asking about her home. The description she gave him was not as sentimental as the one she had shared with Gracie, but her deep and abiding love for Dorio was still plain to see.

Uncle Miltie asked her more about her family's involvement with the Italian partisans. Gracie sensed their history may have been eerily intertwined, perhaps even involving memories too painful for Uncle Miltie to recall.

"My grandmother's sister Constanza," Maddie said, glancing at Uncle Miltie and smiling, "was a messenger for the partisans. She carried directives between groups of them, and had it not been for, ah, her bravery, they could not have communicated.

"She made her way up and down those mountains, always aware that if she were to be caught by Fascists, she would be tortured, probably until death."

Uncle Miltie's expression remained somber. "Brave people. We Americans can't imagine what is like to fight both the invader and the evil force within. Thank God, our country did not have to live it."

"But let us remember and pray for the soldiers who did," Gracie added, as a way of acknowledging her uncle's contribution, along with that of his fallen fellow soldiers and allies.

He nodded, his expression affirming his gratitude for her empathy.

"Nonna's brother is the one in the family who died fighting for liberation," Maddie told them. "He was not much older than me. I wonder of him often. His name was also Giovanni."

Rick put his hand on Maddie's shoulder. "My granddaddy

served in the Pacific. Died there, too. There's a special empti-ness for the soldier who never came home. My grandma mourned his loss all her life."

Maddie's expression was empathetic. "I am sorry."

He rested his hand on her shoulder, as Uncle Miltie flipped through more pages, pointing out locations to Maddie. He was obviously uncomfortable with the direction of the conversation.

He stopped at a photograph of hollow-faced men dressed in rags. "We met them on the road. Jews. They were trying to make their way back to Verona."

But when he turned the page, Maddie said, "Another brother of my grandmother survived a Nazi concentration camp, one of the few who did. Everybody said it was his physical strength that kept him alive. I only remember him as an old man."

Maddie glanced around, realizing they were attracting an audience. Several of the other exchange students were peering at the photographs, and Marge had joined the flock. Maddie blushed, not realizing she'd had an audience for her family story. But Rick coaxed her and Uncle Miltie to tell them more.

"It is my impression," she said, cautiously, "that Italian partisans are often overlooked in history. America is remembered for liberating my country, but they could not have done it so easily had it not been for the partisans."

Uncle Miltie agreed.

"I hope someone has written down your family history, Maddie," Gracie said. She had always wanted to do that, and it saddened her to think how many stories were lost because no one took the time to write them down. She vowed she would not miss the opportunity with George Morgan.

"Perhaps *I* will," Maddie answered.

"And I will, too," Gracie said, eyeing her uncle. She would sit him down some night soon, and record his story on cassette.

Abe and Sophie arrived a little bit later. They had the soup and cheesecakes in several flavors, including pineapple and pumpkin.

A gaggle of kids from the daycare quickly flocked to Abe, eager to touch the black patch he wore over his eye. Gracie wondered if he had replaced the white bandage with something a bit more piratical for this very effect. It was clear to see the deli owner had become the idol of the preschool male set, and he was enjoying the admiration.

"Do you have a wooden leg, too?" one little boy asked incredulously.

Sophie put her hands on her hips. "He *will* have, if he doesn't help carry in those other trays of dessert." She scowled at the children. "I'll feed him to a monster whale, myself."

Eyes grew big and mouths circled in surprise.

Gracie laughed. It was turning out to be a wonderful night!

It was only after the dinner, while folks were milling around selecting among the gooey desserts and browsing the craft tables, that she and Sophie finally had the chance to talk.

"I spoke to Gordon this afternoon," Sophie said, lowering her voice. "I hinted at my frustration with trying to juggle my life in Cleveland and still being on tap for my brother. I just about came out and asked him if I should use my power-of-attorney to sell the place, and force Abe to come to Florida with me. He just said to be patient, he was working on something."

"Did he say what?" Gracie crossed her fingers mentally, hoping for some clue to his true intentions.

She shook her head. "But he did caution me not to talk to people—especially not you!"

"Rocky says he's researching some long-ago glitch in the title process. The way he explains it, all the buyer has to do is declare his intent to purchase, and if no one protests, the property is his."

Sophie caught her breath. It was hard for her to take in. "I don't understand. You're not suggesting he can buy Abe's place out from under him?"

"Perhaps if there is some legal technicality that wasn't met, like an encumbrance on the deed."

Sophie shook her head. "I remember. Abe used part of his inheritance from our grandfather. The lawyer checked. Abe bought from a man who had inherited from his father.

"As I remember, the man didn't have a will, and most of his estate went to settle his debts. The son ended up with what was left—a run-down diner, property the father had simply rented to the operator. The son tried to make a go of it for almost twenty years before Abe bought it. The man was ready to retire."

A wry smile. "To Florida, if I remember correctly. That was 1965. My Henry was still alive, God rest his soul, and wanted to buy property there, saying it was the retirement mecca of the future. If I'd only listened. But the boys were getting older, closer to college age, and we just didn't have the money to spare."

Gracie remembered Ernie Taggart running the diner. She and El had not lived in Willow Bend long when he sold it to Abe. There had been some kind of scandal in the family, but she couldn't remember what.

"Are you sure it isn't the Carruthers place with the deed complication? As I remember, it's been sitting empty for some time now."

Gracie shook her head. John and Maisie had lived in the place as long as she could remember, and now the bank was handling the finances, taxes and such. "It's empty because the Carruthers can't bear to part with it. They love the old place, and I think secretly entertain thoughts of returning." She looked at Sophie. "They never will, though. They're in their nineties, and quite well settled at Pleasant Haven."

It suddenly dawned on Gracie. "Ernie Taggart had a sister."

"Hmm?"

"Yes, she was pregnant and ran off with the father, who had enlisted in the military. He was killed at Normandy, I believe." Gracie met her friend's bewildered gaze. "I knew there was something about the family. I thought it was sad at the time. We lived here when old man Taggart died. If I remember correctly, something was said about him never forgiving her. I think he passed away never having seen his grandchild."

"But what does that have to do with anything?"

Gracie didn't know. It just felt good to recall the story. Her heart went out to Abe, identifying with his frustration. It was like shadow boxing, and Willow Bend was not the kind of place, she felt, where shadows should be at home.

13

GRACIE WAS ON HER WAY to choir practice when Maddie called out to her from the Cantrells' van. "Signora Gracie, do you have a minute?"

She walked around to the passenger side as Maddie climbed out. They exchanged pleasantries, and Maddie thanked her on behalf of her fellow exchange students for the success of the International Fair. She'd brought a book to read for English class while Amy and Linda practiced. They were going to get sandwiches, and do some shopping for school supplies at the mall in Avery after the choir finished.

"Signora, there has been something on your mind, disturbing you, since you asked me about the other accidents."

Maddie's expression was tentative, as if still anticipating distrust. Gracie eased her mind with, "It's all right, dear, we all do impulsive things. The important thing is that you owned up and apologized. You also told Roy and Linda the truth, didn't you?"

She nodded. "I have apologized and apologized to Signor Abe. He is such dear man. His heart is generous. That is why I feel I must say this, even though I am not sure of the meaning."

She had Gracie's attention. "Go on."

"Signor Abe always checks all his burners every night. And everything electrical. He even pulls the plugs. When it was not the case with the coffeepot, I did not have reason to question. I thought I remembered him doing it, but I guessed I must be wrong. Everyone can forget once. I did not defend him, even though my conscience said he was as careful as always.

"I told this to Amy because I feel guilty and did not want to hide *any*thing—*any*more."

She paused, seeming to need affirmation that she was doing the right thing. Gracie rubbed the girl's shoulder. "It's okay, we all forgive you. Please go on."

"Amy remembers that Welty returned her keys one day. He told her he found them in the bathroom. She was happy, because she had missed them the night before. No one knows she had misplaced them. We think that man had her keys that night of the coffeepot."

Maddie leaned on the door. "We wanted to tell you these things, yet feel foolish. As if we have been confusing life with television. Do you think that man could be behind *Signor* Abe's problems?"

"It's beginning to look like that," Gracie confessed. "But we really shouldn't jump to conclusions until we have evidence."

Maddie sighed. "I thought he was a nice man. I told Signor Abe and your uncle how I grew up with my grandmother and did not know my mother or father. Signor Welty was there with Signora Sophie, and he shared with me his own sadness never knowing grandparents, either."

Gracie felt a twinge of sympathy for the man. Perhaps Gordon Welty was not the completely unscrupulous operator she was imagining. *Even villains were once little boys, Lord, I recognize. And maybe he's not a crook, only someone whose actions and motives I'm misunderstanding. It is easy to love those who are kind to us but harder to turn our thoughts lovingly to those who aren't. I pray I'm up to this challenge.*

"*Hmm?*" Maddie was looking at her.

Gracie reached for the door. "Oh, just a dotty old lady talking to the friend in my heart."

"You were talking to God." Maddie smiled. "I like this about you."

They entered the sanctuary, and Maddie opened her palms, seeming to embrace the quietness. "I love this place. It is peaceful, inviting, like the chapel in Dorio."

"The one with the bells?"

Remembrance lit up her face.

Inner beauty, Gracie decided, could be perceived in physical appearance, but was loveliest in moments like this, veiled by humility and devotion. "You are a beautiful young lady."

A blush. Maddie stood beside the back pew. "In Italy, I go to the chapel to light candles in memory of my ancestors, many of them the partisans of whom I have spoken. My grandmother's family. I sit and listen."

"Listen?"

"You were right with your advice, Signora Gracie," she said sliding into the back pew. "Their story should be written down. I will write the story of my family."

She sat and smiled, a twinkle in her blue eyes. "I think you should write yours, too. Begin with Zio Miltie." She giggled. "He asked me to call him Uncle Miltie, too."

Estelle met Gracie at the head of the steps leading into the choir loft. "Barb is in a dither! Sunday night is the concert, and Rick Harding has to go out of town over the weekend."

That was serious. Rick had had extensive choir experience before coming to Willow Bend, and his singing was in the professional category. He usually did the substantial tenor solos, and this piece of music called for a male and female duet with flute accompaniment.

"What are we going to do, Gracie?" Barb exclaimed, coming up beside Estelle. "We only have a couple of days!" She practically glared at Estelle. "I *knew* we shouldn't have tried something so complicated! If we'd just stuck to a simpler, more familiar piece!"

"Yes, yes, keep it simple," Estelle mocked.

Gracie raised her hands in surrender. "Ladies, arguing won't solve our little problem."

"Plain and simple, it's a disaster. We probably will have to sing one of those boring old praise choruses, after all!" Estelle crossed her arms. "Maybe we could still use the flute."

Barb sighed. "What a horrible ending to all our wonderful plans!"

Endings usually come wrapped in new beginnings, Gracie remembered El was fond of saying.

Both women just stared, perhaps waiting to unwrap that which they couldn't yet see. "Why don't we pray about this?" Gracie asked. It seemed the only option she felt appropriate.

Barb and Estelle agreed, and as the choir took their places, they opened in prayer, asking to see a new solution to their dilemma.

"Bert sings tenor," Tish Ball offered and, looking his way, added, "You used to do all the solo parts before we got Rick."

"His voice isn't as disciplined as Rick's," Estelle reasoned without the slightest acrimony in her voice, "but I'm sure he could do the part—it's not *that* hard."

Barb looked at Bert Benton, who stood timidly in the back row.

"You could do it!" Gracie encouraged him, and the others followed suit. Bert was happy to oblige.

Barb stepped back into character as the self-assured choir director, reminding them, "Practice begins promptly at seven, not one minute after or a moment before." She tapped her music stand. "Please follow me."

Estelle sought Gracie out after choir practice. Marge excused herself, flashing Gracie a "you-poor-thing" look. Gracie couldn't help recalling Estelle's assessment of Amy's problem. Could she, Gracie, by the same token, unconsciously be shutting this woman out? She was close to most of the other members, it was true, and they often chatted afterwards, yet often Estelle disappeared right after practice.

"Marge, stay. We'll all walk out together."

Estelle looked at Gracie, her eyes questioning.

Gracie returned her stare.

"I wanted to talk about our hypothesis—you know, the one we discussed on our walk."

"Welty?"

Estelle nodded, her expression conveying caution.

"Marge has the same suspicions as we do," Gracie told her. "I haven't shared everything, so we can update her as we walk."

Estelle seemed genuinely pleased to be included for a change. Gracie realized that Estelle may never have chosen to hang around after practice simply because she didn't feel part of the easy camaraderie of the others. Gracie made a note to talk to Marge later about changing that situation.

Afterward, Gracie updated Marge on the conversation she and Estelle had shared.

"I went to see Avis at the courthouse today," Estelle told them. "She was curious, and checked to see which file Welty had asked her to copy."

Gracie's interest piqued. "And?"

"It was Gordon Taggart's."

Marge's mouth circled in surprise. "You mean Ernest Taggart. Ernie owned the diner back in the sixties."

Estelle hesitated. "Maybe she made a mistake and combined the two names. The important thing is that *both* the Carruthers place and the diner were owned by Taggart."

"I hadn't realized," Gracie thought out loud. "Did you know that, Marge? You've lived in this town all of your life."

"Ernie's grandfather was one of the early settlers, I remember that. He owned a lot of property, but lost most of it during the Depression. All that was before my day." Marge patted her hair. "Remember, I'm even younger than you!" She laughed. "No, seriously. *I* don't know much about the history of the town—but I can guess who does."

"Cordelia!" They said in unison.

"Good night!" Barb waved from her car. "See you Sunday morning!"

Marybeth stopped to chat, pleased that Bert could pinch-hit for Rick. Gracie wasn't paying close attention, however, as her mind was on this latest development. She planned to call Rocky as soon as she got the chance.

She left a message for him on his voice mail, but he turned out to be in her own garage when she got home. Of course, she had to park Fannie Mae in the driveway and use the side door, because Uncle Miltie still didn't have the new opener operational.

"Why didn't you answer your cell phone?" She asked Rocky.

Rocky unsnapped the thing from his belt. "I don't always hear the ringer."

Uncle Miltie shook his head. "You better get a hearing aid, and hope a big story doesn't break before you do!"

"You better keep your thoughts on that instruction sheet!"

Gracie gave the time-out signal. "I *know* I don't have to ask if you're hungry! I've got some leftover desserts from International Night at the church. What do you say?"

"You don't have to ask twice."

Over coffee and slices of Abe's cheesecake, Gracie filled them in on the day's unravelings.

"Ann O'Neil might have a conflict of interest if anything comes of this," Rocky was saying. "She's the attorney for John and Maisie. I think we need to have a talk with her, update her on what we know."

Uncle Miltie rubbed his chin. "So if Ernie Taggart didn't have clear title when he sold the place to Welty, then technically Abe doesn't own it."

"Looks that way," Rocky said. "But neither do John and Maisie Carruthers, if what Estelle says is true."

Gracie sighed, thinking of the couple in the nursing home who dreamed of returning to a house they couldn't maintain. That run-down place remained their hope—the hope that they would once again be able to take care of themselves. "The bank is taking care of the taxes. I know they set up a trust. Wouldn't someone at the bank see the problem with the deed?"

"Nobody checked," Rocky said. "That couple lived in that house longer than Abe's owned the deli! Who would have had reason to check if there was another inheritor?"

That piqued Gracie's interest. "Another inheritor?"

"Uh-huh, isn't that what we are assuming? Ernie's father left him those places in his will. You remember a sister?"

But she wasn't remembering it all. There was more to it, she was sure. "The sister was estranged. She ran away with a soldier. I don't think the father ever forgave her, and I don't remember her coming back." She looked at Rocky. "And I can't remember where I heard the story. Maybe it was gossip."

Gracie felt ashamed, realizing how often she had succumbed to listening to juicy tidbits from the lives of other people, particularly back in her younger days.

Rocky studied Gracie over the top of his coffee mug. "I think I remember your telling me Taggart was dead. But is there anyone still alive? That person could answer all our questions."

"He and Mary didn't have children." She paused, recalling, "I think she's still alive. She came back here from Florida and lives with her sister over in Coltrain, I believe. Cordelia Fountain will know that, too."

"Too?" Rocky eyed her.

"Oh, the strangest thing—Avis Murphy gave the name *Gordon* Taggart as owner of the properties in the 1920s. We want to check on that name. She could have unconsciously combined it with Welty's—or, if she didn't. . . ." She met Rocky's gaze. "You don't suppose Ernie's father's name was *Gordon*?"

Gracie had an uncanny feeling that there was something she wasn't remembering. That elusive memory swam up in her mind, teasingly close to the surface; but just when she reached out to catch it, like quicksilver it slipped from view.

"My memory box!" Gracie excused herself to retrieve her box of newspaper clippings. She'd faithfully kept newspaper clippings of births, weddings, obituaries and other articles of interest about people she cared about. She and El had attended Ernie's funeral. El had played golf with the man.

Uncle Miltie seemed genuinely interested in her collection,

asking questions about friends as she went through the stack. Rocky looked at feature stories with his byline. "You've got a regular archival library, Gracie."

"Snippets of Willow Bend history now," she agreed. "Aged and fragile." Not unlike themselves. She looked down at the front-page headline on El's accident. "Important, all the same."

The box of printed memories documented her journey, both the joy and the heartbreak. She folded that most painful memory, and tucked it away under the stack. Rocky put his hand on hers.

She smiled at him, as they shared a moment of companionable silence, remembering the very special man whom they both, in their different ways, had cherished.

She returned her focus to the collection, retrieving Ernie's obituary. She scanned the column. He had passed away in Florida where he had retired.

Ernie Taggart had been well-respected. In a little feature article accompanying the obituary they read this quote from his wife, "He always wanted to be reunited with his sister and her son. My husband especially wanted his nephew to have his grandfather's pocket watch. He did all he could to find Kathryn, but she seems to have disappeared from the face of the earth."

She felt a tightness in her throat. "Ernie *did* have a sister— Kathryn, who apparently had a son. *Gordon?*"

The day had been both unsettled and unsettling, so after Rocky left and Uncle Miltie had gone to bed, Gracie sat with her box of memories, and drank a mug of warm milk. She talked to El about the kids, telling him again about their wonderful grandson. She thought of Gordon Taggart's missing that opportunity.

Oh, Lord, what stubborn creatures we can be.

"I don't have a conflict of interest," Ann O'Neil told them. "Gordon Welty isn't my client. It seemed like he was going to ask me to represent him, but he never followed through."

Rocky stroked his chin, apparently thinking things through. "So you think the guy has a legal leg to stand on?"

"Yes, he does. And since the case is so old, I doubt whether there's even any inheritance tax to be paid. I'll have to do some research. I'm going to call Abe right after you leave. He ought to know what he's facing, especially if Welty's planning a civil suit."

Gracie couldn't help but feel a twinge of sympathy for the man. "Don't you think he can be reasoned with?"

"He's nothing but an opportunist!" Rocky exclaimed.

"What businessman isn't?" she reminded him. "Plus, he's human, too. He may believe he has reason to hate this town and us. Yet, he's agreed to donate money for our town's historical projects. Surely he can't be all bad?"

Rocky harrumphed. "Bribery. He wants that parking lot."

Ann tapped her pencil on her pad. "I think I'll call the bank about the Carruthers, too. That house is all they have! They turned most of their other assets over to the nursing home."

"Still think he's interested in anyone but himself?" Rocky teased Gracie. "Not everybody has a conscience."

But they did have a prayer! That she knew, for sure.

THINGS CAME TO A HEAD the very next day, when Abe received notification from the sheriff's office that Gordon Welty was indeed filing a suit in civil court, an Action to Quiet Title. He, in fact, *was* the son of Kathryn Taggart.

"Thirty-five years of my life!" Abe said, waving the paper. "Meaningless! How can he do this?"

Sophie's eyes were red and swollen. "I am sorry I ever met the man." She looked at Gracie. "Tell my brother, I only wanted the best for him! How could I have known?"

"Sophie, leave it to me now," Abe ordered her. "You meant well, I know."

Sophie pleaded, "Please, Gracie, make him understand that he needs me beside him!"

Rocky interrupted. "Welty has filed a civil action. So what? These cases could take years, especially if they're contested."

He focused his gaze on Abe. "And you *are* going to contest!"

"Of course I am going to fight!" Abe straightened. "This is my life. This my delicatessen!" To Sophie. "I don't want to live in Florida! Even if I can't spell my name or recognize myself in the mirror, I want to stay right here in Willow Bend!"

Sophie started to cry, and Maddie came forward to comfort her. Gracie looked at Amy, whose expression was stricken. She was only a teenager, but she cared deeply about her friend and employer. It seemed that the worst of situations brought out the best in good people. Character was not built, but was revealed under pressure. Gracie was proud of her friends, who used love as the building blocks of their relationships and who never seemed to stint on it, as if their supply was limitless.

She sent a prayer heavenward.

"Have you talked to Ann O'Neil?" Rocky asked.

Abe shook his head. "I just got this thing a half-hour ago." And, handing it to Rocky to look at, he said, "You and Gracie have come at just the right time, the way you always do."

"I did talk to my lawyer," offered Sophie, dabbing her eyes with a tissue. "After Gracie told me what Welty could be planning, I called him and asked if he would inquire around. He also had heard allegations that Gordon wasn't averse to taking advantage of gullible women like me."

Abe reassured her. "You're not gullible, Sophie. You've got

a trusting heart, that's all. You're a shrewd businesswoman, and I respect you for that."

"Thank you." Sophie and her brother gazed solemnly at each other for a long moment, and Gracie quietly thanked God for working in their midst.

"So what did your lawyer suggest?" Rocky wanted to know. He handed the document back to Abe.

Sophie straightened, pulling herself together. "Welty had advised me to liquidate some stock and invest in his venture. I did what he asked. I wrote him a check for the amount of the transfer." She was clearly embarrassed. "I invested in his venture before I even talked to my brother."

She looked at Abe. "The condominium in Florida seemed perfect for us. I'm so sorry." She turned to the others. "Several women in my investment group gave him money. My lawyer says we need to check into exactly where those funds went."

"Are you willing to appear against him?" Rocky asked. "If he's charged with fraud in your case, you will probably have to testify in court."

Gracie still couldn't believe what was happening. "Even if he hasn't done anything blatantly illegal, maybe the threat of a counter-suit will be enough to get him to drop the one against Abe. Maybe the possibility of a little adverse publicity won't fit in with his expansion plans."

Sophie set her jaw. "I'll do whatever it takes to help Abe. I got him into this mess."

It was Abe who reached out this time. While they hugged each other, Gracie put her arms around Maddie and Amy. "What others intend for evil, God transforms. He works all things for good for those who love Him."

"Even with my mother?" Maddie's voice was barely audible.

Surprised, Gracie squeezed her shoulders. "I'm sure of it," she whispered, praying she was right. Maddie's interest in her mother was a sign—and a positive one.

Coltrain was their first stop, where Gracie, Sophie, Amy and Maddie intended to rattle some closet skeletons, and then perhaps put them to rest at last. They were going to visit Ernie's widow and her sister. After that they planned to go to Cleveland together, where Maddie, her heart now softened, suddenly understood it was important to visit her mother.

Mary Taggart patted her sister Emily's hand. "Ernie was a good man. But everything was business with Gordon, just like with my father. And he had a hard heart."

Emily nodded her head, remembering along with her sister. Gracie thought perhaps she'd heard it many times before.

"Ernie's sister Kathryn fell in love. Gordon did not like the boy because he came from *ordinary* stock. He refused their marriage and was threatening to send Kathryn away. But she ran off before he had time to follow through."

She sighed. "It's a sad, sad story. I married Ernie the following spring. His father had disowned Kathryn by then."

"We do stupid things," Emily said. "Fortunately, the good Lord forgives us our foolishness. Repeatedly." Amy and Maddie giggled.

"Gordon simply never found it in his heart to forgive Kathryn. She wrote him a letter, saying he had a grandson and that her husband had been killed in France. Gordon tore it into pieces." Mary looked past them, as though seeing that time. "I watched him do it—I begged him to answer it—to tell her to come home. He threw the letter into the fire.

"I cried as I watched it burn. I cried for Ernie, and prayed for his father's soul."

The lines around Mary's eyes softened, as she turned her attention back to the present with a doleful smile. "Ernie wanted desperately to know his sister's son. All of his life, he waited for a letter that didn't come.

"His father died a few years later. What with hospital debts, there wasn't much left of the estate. Ernie was left with property: the family home, the house on Cherry and the restaurant. The Carruthers had been renting the house for years. Gordon had bought that place for his parents and then, when they passed on, he rented it. He had always intended to move into town one day, but he never did."

She offered them more tea, and when she'd poured it, she continued. "By that time, we'd fixed up the apartment above the diner, suspecting we were not going to have children. Selling the other properties to cover debts made sense, but Ernie loved that diner. He was a darling man, the perfect husband! Not at all like his father.

"He didn't have grand aspirations. He didn't want anything his father had to give him. He never forgave Gordon for driving Kathryn away. Oh, he was there for his father, don't get me wrong—but underneath there was an ache, a disappointment that just wouldn't heal. He had heart problems, you know. In more ways than one, I suppose."

She dabbed her eyes with a linen handkerchief. "Tell Kathryn's son I'd like to meet him, for Ernie's sake."

"It's a shame we punish each other with our pain," Emily said. "How much easier it would be to bear, if we were only willing to share. . . ."

Mary handed Gracie the pocket watch. "For Gordon, in case he can't forgive either."

Arriving at Sophie's comfortable house in the Cleveland suburbs, Maddie called her mother. Amy stood next to her, while Gracie and Sophie exchanged enigmatic glances. Although Maddie didn't say much, her voice was soft and calm. She even smiled at one point in the conversation. Then she passed the phone so Sophie could give directions.

"We could bring Maddie to you," she said to the woman on the phone.

Maddie shook her head. Apparently, the mother agreed with her daughter. Sophie gave directions. "Okay, an hour then. We look forward to meeting you." She hung up the phone and turned to Maddie. "This is going to be tough. You could have her come in and visit with you here. It might be easier having friends around."

"It's something we have to do alone. You both have been Nonna to me. I feel her smile in heaven to see I am taken care of in such a way. I thank you both for this."

She hugged Amy, then Sophie. Gracie felt tears well as Maddie hugged her next.

Patrizia English arrived less than an hour later. She was a small woman with dark features and brooding eyes, like Maddie but not like Maddie. She fidgeted with the silk scarf around her neck. Gracie thought she seemed much older than her actual age. There were deep creases at her mouth and fine lines at the corners of her eyes, which were accentuated by heavy make-up.

Sophie was gracious, inviting her to stay for supper, but she politely refused. Maddie stayed close to her, and Gracie appreciated Abe's sister's diplomacy as she kept the conversation moving past awkward moments. Sophie discovered Patrizia had had no other children, and that her husband was in a wheelchair, suffering through the last stages of multiple sclerosis. To be a caregiver in such a situation was no simple matter, Gracie understood.

After Patrizia and Maddie left to spend some time alone together, Gracie lowered her head to pray. Sophie sat down beside her, patting the seat next to her for Amy to occupy.

"Our young friend here has been keeping quiet as all this drama unfolds. But I know Maddie has been grateful that you wanted to come with her." She watched Amy for a moment or so, as the girl looked around the room.

Gracie said suddenly, "I have a good feeling about this. Especially after Mary gave me Gordon's pocket watch to give his grandson. It may even bring the peace for which I think that man is really looking. I think deep down, love and acceptance is all any of us desire. That's all Maddie was looking for."

Sophie nodded. "Sweet girl. Girls," she corrected herself. She then sighed deeply. "I've never been close to my daughters-in-law. I couldn't help seeing myself in Mary's story about Welty's grandfather."

She met Gracie's gaze. "So how is it that this Italian teenager melts my heart, *hmm*?" Her expression sombered. "I always wanted a daughter, and my mother was Italian."

"I guess that's it," Gracie laughed affectionately. "Case solved."

She then sighed. "Kids. I guess the important thing always is to know when to let go of them."

"*Hmm?*"

"And learn to love the ones our loved ones bring home to us. I often heard El's mother say, when asked about me, her daughter-in-law, that she only had children, no in-laws."

Sophie smiled. "That's nice. I remember you once referred to her as the mother of your heart."

Recalling that gave Gracie a warm feeling and, sipping tea, she savored the memory of her mentor. "I guess until we love those children, we'll be on the outside. Daughters don't have to be flesh and blood."

Sophie concurred. "Maddie has taught us that, hasn't she?"

Gracie looked thoughtful.

Amy said, "I think there are many definitions of family— and we're always learning new ones. Maddie feels like my sister now . . . so I guess you're both my adopted grandmas, as well."

They all laughed.

Later that night, Patrizia dropped her daughter off at Sophie's without coming in. Maddie joined Amy, Gracie and Sophie in the kitchen, but did not say much about her meeting with her mother, except that Patrizia would like to visit Willow Bend sometime. Gracie took this as a sign that further reconciliation lay ahead, and told Maddie she'd be happy to have her mother stay with her, should she make the journey.

"Would you like some hot chocolate?" Sophie asked, getting up from the table. "My children used to love it."

Maddie and Amy agreed that it sounded delicious. "Did you find anything more about Mr. Welty and your money?" Maddie asked Sophie. Amy listened, her expression troubled. All of them had a stake in the outcome of Sophie and Abe's problems.

"I have an appointment in the morning before we return to Willow Bend," Sophie said. "But my broker says Welty's venture looks good on paper." Sophie smiled wryly. "He thinks the fellow is on the up-and-up this time, so I probably don't have a case. I don't know if that is bad or good."

Maddie accepted a mug of steaming cocoa. "What will you do if there is no case? Can you make Welty give you back your money?"

Sophie shrugged. "I don't know what options I have until I talk to my lawyer. Hopefully, Welty will drop the lawsuit."

Sophie handed another mug to Amy. "I may not have gotten anything illegal on Welty, but this trip has had special meaning for me.

"I'm glad I helped make this meeting with your mother

possible," she told Maddie. "I know you feel disappointed I'm not staying in Willow Bend. But please remember that wherever I am, my home is yours."

"Thank you," Maddie said softly, her face still showing the strain. "I have been angry with my mother all of my life. She wanted to come to Italy when my nonna died, but she could not leave her husband for so long. She called me the day of the funeral, but I would not talk to her. . . . I wanted to talk to her, but the anger was a barrier stronger than love. And the love, it was too weak to surmount it."

Maddie remained quiet a long moment. "And, so, between us was only silence . . . and my anger. Now . . . I am glad you encouraged me to do this. It was time."

Gracie patted Maddie's hand. "It is what God has been wanting, I know."

"My mother told me today that she wrote many letters, but I did not ever reply. She said she invited me to come live with her here in the United States, but Nonna assured her I did not want anything to do with her."

Maddie had tears in her eyes. "I do not know what to believe. Nonna told me my mother never wrote. I know she telephoned, because Nonna Ida would get very upset. Yet had I talked to her, it would have angered and hurt my grandmother. I feel uncertain about what I should do now."

"Your mother is alive," Gracie said, softly. "Your grandmother is not. Whatever was between them perhaps should stay buried. Try to accept the friendship your mother is offering—it's probably all she has to give right now. It must also be hard for her. Don't expect too much, too soon. Don't expect answers she may not even have for a long time."

Maddie looked up. "But what about my grandmother? My mother hurt her terribly! She ran away—left me."

Gracie prayed for wisdom. "Your mother made mistakes," she began, searching for the right words. "But whatever happened between your mother and grandmother in the past is not as important as the future.

"You must accept this opening as a gift—to both you and your mother." Gracie squeezed her hand. "If you'll let God help you heal, I think you and your mother will build a wonderful relationship, perhaps stronger than any you could have imagined. He cannot give back the lost years, but He holds the key to every satisfaction that lays ahead."

Sophie cautioned, "But don't expect too much. Forgiveness takes time. You both have to build trust in one another."

"This I understand," Maddie said. "I knew it was right to make peace with my mother when I heard the story of Kathryn and her father. I told my mother that story."

"Remember," Sophie said. "Forgiveness is risky business. Either one of you can pull out at any time and the other would be left hurting. Both of you need each other's support—and courage."

Amy nodded. "I think you will be stronger for this now, Maddie dear. Strong for you and strong for your mother."

"We did not talk of the past," Maddie added softly. "I wanted to know why she left me, but I was afraid to ask. We talked of Italy and the family, not important things. She is like a stranger . . . but not a stranger."

Maddie smiled at Gracie. "She remembers Dorio, and you are right, Signora Gracie, she has often longed to go home."

Gracie couldn't help wondering if God wasn't using this time to make that journey possible. She would pray for mother and daughter, and the small steps they were taking in the direction of one another. *Only You, dear Lord, are the perfect guide for them as they embark on this blessed path.*

ANN O'NEILL HAD SCHEDULED a meeting with Gordon Welty, and Abe already was beside himself with anticipation when Gracie dropped Sophie off.

"She says we have the trump card!" Abe's voice was puzzled. "I was never any good at cards. I've never understood the rules. I don't understand the rules now! How can someone attempt to lay claim to a property someone else has owned for almost half his life?"

"What's even stranger, though, is that he doesn't have a lawyer," Abe told them. "He's done all the research with the help of a paralegal—Rocky thinks it's because he doesn't want unnecessary paperwork. He thought he could pull this off with that Action to Quiet Title."

He was pacing now. "He makes a claim, shows the judge

the will and proof he is the heir, and the judge rules in his favor, thinking there are no contesting parties. That's why he put such a tiny ad in the paper. He didn't count on Eagle Eye Gravino, I can tell you that!"

"So what is this trump card?" Sophie asked.

Abe shook his head. "Ann didn't tell me. All she said was to have Gracie and Rocky speak for my character, and to attest to the fact I have been sole owner and operator of this place."

"I still think I should call my lawyer," Sophie proposed. "He has a few questions of his own to ask Gordon Welty! If the man is going to have shareholders—as I and my friends evidently are—he must follow the proper legal procedures, and my lawyer suspects that's not the case."

Abe sat down and lowered his head. "I've been sick over this. Today I wish I could forget! Forget my worries, that is what I wish—but no, they plague me! Every little detail looms large, suffocating me."

He looked at Gracie. "Maybe I *am* losing my mind."

"Tell me about the photographs," Gracie said, pointing to the collection on the table beside him, and hoping to ease his mind. "I know you've told me before, but I forget."

He picked up a leather frame. "My parents, may they rest in peace. And that is Mike on my mother's lap." He smiled. "Sophie is beside her, and me next to my father."

Gracie bent closer to admire Sophie as a pre-adolescent

with bobbed hair. Abe looked somber, as though trying to appear the little man of the family. Mike was a chubby boy of about four.

"These are my mother's grandparents—Bernardo and Leah Benevisti."

"What handsome people," she told him.

"They came to the United States in the early twenties. They could feel an eerie stillness between the wars—the calm before the storm, which was not so calm in Italy. When Mussolini came to power, they were sure they had to leave. They left their family in Italy and came to Chicago."

Gracie studied the photograph. "What happened to the family? You told me that your mother's brother escaped to France with the help of partisans. How about the rest of the family?"

"Some were deported to German camps, although none of my immediate family. Others went into hiding, and many joined the partisans. My grandparents died the year I was born—1928. Thanks be they never knew the horror that would unfold in the years to follow."

He sighed and took the photograph back. "My grandparents did not live very far from Maddie's home in Italy. Perhaps it was one of her relatives who helped our family."

"The world *is* really very small, isn't it?" Sophie said, sitting on the edge of her brother's chair. "And for a world with so many inhabitants, it is amazing how lives cross—even through generations."

Gracie nodded, thinking of Gordon Welty and Ernie Taggart; Maddie's mother living so close to Sophie, and of Uncle Miltie with photographs of villages that were familiar to Maddie. It almost seemed as if all roads led to Willow Bend. She thought of Uncle Miltie and his Italian compatriot enjoying the cigar. From Italy to Indiana: there seemed to be some meaning to these connections and Gracie trusted it would soon be revealed to her.

Sophie picked up a newer photo showing her with her two brothers in front of a different deli. "Our German grandfather ran a deli, and our Italian grandfather was an intellectual."

"Typical Americans!" Abe laughed.

Sophie leaned her head against his. "We have much to cope with and I'm tired." Her mood seemed to have shifted.

"I am, too," Abe said. He glanced protectively at his sister.

Gracie went home, confident that her friends would get a good night's sleep and that things would look brighter in the morning. *Best of all, Lord,* she noted, *they are in harmony again.*

By the time Gracie and Rocky arrived at the courthouse the next morning, Abe and Welty were already at logger-heads. Abe was accusing his adversary of sabotage, while Gordon Welty was hardly bothering to be polite when it came to Abe's presumed competence. Ann, to no avail, was trying to interject the voice of reason. A nervous young man, undoubtedly the paralegal Welty had hired, sat in the corner, hugging a stack of papers.

"Gracie!" Ann exclaimed, and the room got quiet.

Abe stood to greet them, explaining to Rocky that Welty had made it plain that he believed he was doing Abe a good turn. "Saving me from myself, I suppose!" He glared around the room, as if daring anyone to agree.

Gracie cleared her throat. "I hope we can work this out. I've spent some time with Mary Taggart, and I believe I can speak to her belief that her late husband would want to do right by his nephew."

Welty furrowed his brow. "You spent time with whom?"

"Your Uncle Ernie's widow. She now lives in Coltrain with her sister. She sends you her regards."

Abe took a seat, his expression unsure. Sophie had been sitting quietly at the table and now patted her brother's hand reassuringly.

"You're looking for an equitable solution, aren't you? There may be a way. . . ."

"I just want to keep what is mine," Abe asserted.

Rocky stared at Gracie, obviously perplexed.

Lord, we need Your wisdom and impartiality. Gracie felt calm. It would turn out all right, if they would only listen to one another. And not just listen, but hear.

Ann squared the papers on the table in front of her. "If we'd all just take a seat, we'll get started. This is just an informal meeting to see if we can reach a compromise."

Abe shook a finger. "I'm not compromising my deed."

"The deed is not legal," Welty reiterated. "Ernest Taggart sold that property which my mother had equal claim on, without her knowledge or consent."

Rocky cleared his throat. "There was no will, I checked."

"That's part of the problem," Ann said. "Ernest shouldn't have inherited alone. It was assumed he was the only heir. His sister Kathryn wasn't here, but that doesn't mean she lost her rights. In fact, she inherited with Ernest, because there was no will to the contrary."

She looked at Welty. "Technically, this does not qualify as a Quiet Title Action, and you know it. That procedure presumes all concerned parties are deceased, and that there is no way to negotiate a deed transaction."

"That will be for a judge to decide." Welty was indignant. "My mother was cheated out of her rightful inheritance."

Abe threw his hands up. "I didn't cheat anyone! I paid a fair price."

"Let me get something straight," Rocky said to Welty, "as long as we're talking wrongful behavior here. Do you deny setting Abe up to look like he was forgetful, perhaps developing dementia?"

Welty ignored him, and turned to face Ann. "I think I'd

like to take my chances with a judge, unless you've got a compromise that involves reimbursing me for my mother's life." He paused, his voice cracking a little. "She's the real victim here."

"I can't be held responsible for someone else's family problems," Abe protested. "I bought that property fair and square. I invested thirty-five years of my life in it."

"That is exactly the point." Ann read from the sheet of paper in front of her. "You have openly operated under the premise that this was, in fact, your property. There is a legal precedent for it: it is called 'adverse possession.' That is why I asked Gracie and Rocky here as witnesses to your character, and to attest to the fact that you have been operating a business on that property continuously for the last—"

"Thirty-five years!" Abe reiterated.

Ann looked at Welty. "There are plenty of people in Willow Bend who are willing to swear to Abe's good intentions, and to the fact that he has been there for—" she smiled at Abe, "almost thirty-five years."

"My mother's memory is worth more to me than all his good intentions!" Welty's jaw was set. "She struggled all of her life, finally dying of cancer. I want her to get what is rightfully hers."

Sophie now spoke up. "It's my belief you happened across that information accidentally! If you hadn't been looking for a loophole—a way to cheat Abe out of what is *rightfully* his, your mother would still be resting in peace. The way it stands now, she'd probably be ashamed of you!"

Both men sat down, still glaring at one another.

It was Gracie who broke the angry silence. "Gentlemen, we're reasonable people. Let's listen to what Mrs. O'Neill has to say."

Ann leaned forward. "I know there is a group of women in Cleveland who are considering filing a suit against you, Mr. Welty. Sophie's lawyer called me."

The man's jaw remained set, but he pushed the knuckles of one hand with the other.

"Mr. Welty, it seems Mrs. Glass and her friends may be able to keep you in legal binds for who knows how long—perhaps long enough for you to lose this business opportunity."

She looked at Sophie. "But Mrs. Glass is a gracious woman and has agreed to withdraw her suit if you do the same with the one against her brother. The investment group will settle for fair compensation for what they have already invested.

"This is more than reasonable, considering the aggravation you have caused them." She eyed Welty again.

Welty didn't say anything for a long moment.

"I'm going to fight you every step of the way," Abe reminded him. "I'll go kicking and punching into the grave if that's what it takes. But you'll never get my deli!"

Welty stayed quiet.

"It is surely no credit to your mother's memory that you

used me to hurt my brother." Sophie gave a Abe a rueful side glance.

"I'm ashamed of myself for ever doubting his mental capacity." She focused her attention back on Welty. "And if I could prove you did any of those things, I'd see you behind bars. But I can't. And obviously you are not man enough to admit what you've done."

Sophie let out a deep sigh. "I will not only drop the civil suit, but I will write off my investment with you, as long as you take your business interests somewhere else. If your franchise does work out and you feel an ounce of remorse, you can give my profit to charity."

"I won't have you taken advantage of!" Abe was on his feet. "He bamboozled us and shouldn't benefit to the tune of a single penny. Not a red cent!"

If only she could call a truce for prayer, Gracie thought. Just for a few minutes—time enough to ask the Lord to be the arbitrater.

But You're already here, aren't You? Where two or more are gathered, You are in their midst. Oh, Father, give us accord. Help us to resolve this horrible situation.

Then she remembered the pocket watch and the newspaper clipping, both still in her pocketbook. Whispering, "Thank You," she quietly retrieved them.

"Your uncle wanted you to have this," she said to Welty as she stood to hand over to him what she'd been keeping.

"Ernie Taggart regretted never having the opportunity to give it to you personally, as you'll plainly see if you read the last paragraphs of his obituary."

Gordon held the watch gingerly in one hand, turning it over and over in his palm, and not saying anything while he read the story.

Gracie was thankful that the reporter had written with his heart, finding the human interest angle. If it hadn't been for the poignancy of those last paragraphs, Gracie probably would never have remembered Kathryn's story.

"Your grandfather died an unhappy man," Sophie said. "Isn't that enough? None of us wants that for our loved ones—yet when we have the conviction that we have been wronged, it is natural to feel otherwise."

Gracie looked at her friend. Sophie's expression revealed compassion for her enemy. *Lord, You certainly are in our midst.*

"Your uncle wanted to know you," Gracie told him. "He loved your mother very much. All his life he longed to be reunited with her, but she never contacted him. I guess it was not to be."

Gordon rubbed his thumb over the engraved initials. "This is really my grandfather's watch? He wanted *me* to have it?"

Gracie nodded her head, deciding not to remind him that it was Ernie who really had wanted his nephew to have the heirloom.

"You ought to go visit your Aunt Mary," Sophie told him

gently. "She's such a lovely woman. She would welcome seeing you."

He met Sophie's gaze. "I don't know what to say."

"Life is too short for anger, grudges and bitterness." She shook her head. "My grandfather used to say that everybody has a swan moment. We are all born ugly ducklings, feeling like misfits most of our lives. But there comes a magic moment when we do something grand—wonderful, benevolent beyond reason. It is at that moment we are transformed. Perhaps this is yours. . . .

"You can't change the past . . . but you can make the future better." She moved to stand behind her brother. "We don't want to cheat you, Gordon. We're honest folks—ordinary people. We're not rich materially, but in spirit our wealth is beyond imagination. We want to do right by you."

She beamed at them all and leaned over to kiss her brother. "Don't we, Abe?"

He grumbled but patted her hand. "Yes, of course we do."

"This isn't the ending I expected," Gordon said softly.

Gracie brushed tears from her eyes. "God has a habit of wrapping endings in wonderful new beginnings!" she reminded them.

"What's today's blue-plate special?" Rocky asked, moseying up to the counter beside Gracie. The sun was streaming in the front window. Gracie glanced at it for an instant, admiring it as she always did.

Abe reached for two coffee cups. "Same as always, with free advice on the side."

"What if I don't want the advice?"

Abe laughed. "You get it anyway. I'm a *sage*, remember? We get to say whatever we want, and you young pups have to listen. That's the way it works."

"What do you hear from Sophie?" Gracie asked.

Abe shook his head. "Sophie is Sophie. That woman never learns her lesson. She's sending me brochures on cruises now. I'll get a break at least when she goes off to stay with her sons, first one, then the other. She probably wants them to retire with us, too, so she can reduce her travel time!"

Chuckling, he poured her coffee. "I hear Maddie's mother is coming for a visit, and that she is staying with you."

"Yes, I think they've got a chance to rebuild their relationship from the ground up. It may be awkward for a while, but some day, after her husband has passed on," Gracie thought out loud, "I imagine Patrizia will return to Italy."

Gracie thought how different it could have turned out if Maddie hadn't taken that first step. "For now, God had given mother and daughter time to get to know each other, and friends to support them through the difficult reunion process."

Abe paused, perhaps also thinking of Gordon Welty. Gracie wished things could have been different for him. At least Welty had gone to meet Mary and started his own path to reconciliation.

In fact, he had left Willow Bend almost as abruptly as he had arrived. He had dropped the suit, giving up his claims to both properties although he never admitted to staging Abe's accidents. That was hardly surprising, Gracie knew, and his silence in this instance spoke the proverbial volumes.

It would be months or longer until Sophie and the women of her investment club actually untangled their dealings with Welty. That was too bad, but Gracie's hopeful compassion made her wish he'd understood the swan moment offered him for the important opportunity it was.

She would continue to pray that Gordon Welty's change of heart was a lasting one. Why shouldn't receiving that pocket watch and meeting Mary Taggart have made all the difference? *Lord, with Your watching over him, I know it must have.*

"Did Uncle Miltie get that glitch fixed in the new garage-door opener?" Rocky wanted to know, as he poured cream in his coffee. "I told him that it's the sensor. He definitely should have bought the better model, but there's no reasoning with him when he thinks he's found a bargain."

"It still goes berserk when you get within a foot of the

electronic eye," she told him. "Then it makes a horrible whirling noise before finally going up."

Rocky grinned. "So what's for supper? This editor—I mean handyman—doesn't work cheap."

Gracie shook her head, and laughed. "Meat loaf and scalloped potatoes."

"We might have it repaired by the first snowfall. How's that sound?"

She gave him a thumbs-up. "At least the Pearly Gates are still manually operated, so far as we know," she teased.

It was good to be home.

Gracie's Deluxe Three-Bean Salad

- ✓ One 14½-ounce can green beans
- ✓ One 14½-ounce can wax beans
- ✓ One 14½-ounce can kidney beans
- ✓ One to two 4-ounce jars diced pimientos
- ✓ 1 cup chopped onion
- ✓ 1 cup chopped celery

- ✓ 1/2 cup salad oil
- ✓ 3/4 cup vinegar
- ✓ 1 cup sugar
- ✓ 1 tablespoon water
- ✓ 1 teaspoon salt
- ✓ 1 teaspoon pepper
- ✓ 1 small green pepper, finely chopped

Empty each can of beans into a colander and rinse well, to remove the "canned" taste. Pat the beans with paper towels and set aside in colander to dry. When they seem dry enough, put them into a large bowl with pimientos and vegetables, and mix well. In a saucepan, heat oil, vinegar, sugar, water, and salt and pepper over low heat until the sugar melts. Pour this liquid over vegetables, and blend well. Cover and set in refrigerator, and let stand overnight. Drain well and serve at room temperature.

Gracie says, "For an extra bit of texture and flavor, I like to add a can of white corn to the vegetable blend. But remember to rinse and dry these little nuggets well, too!"

"I, like Gracie, love homemaking and cooking," writes ROBERTA UPDEGRAFF. "I married my high-school sweetheart, have been married for more than twenty-five years and have three-plus wonderful children. I say plus because our home seems to sprout teenagers and young adults, making our dinner table banter quite lively.

"I am a substitute teacher at Williamsport High School in Pennsylvania, and I love my students! This year I'm teaching drama. I have taught everything from auto mechanics to orchestra. I am also a Sunday school teacher and youth leader. Obviously, I enjoy teenagers.

"Like the Meyers in *The Un-nimble Thimble*, another Guideposts 'Church Choir Mysteries,' my husband and I responded to the news reports of Hurricane Mitch, and felt God calling us to offer friendship and labor. We have participated in two work trips to Honduras, and this year we were joined by our youngest daughter and an Italian exchange student. I took puppets and lots of books to work with the children. Next year we're planning to drive a school bus loaded with needed supplies.

"I am a member of the St. David's Christian Writers' Conference board of directors, and I am active in West Branch Christian Writers. Although this is my second book, I have sold numerous articles to publications like *Moody*, *Focus on the Family*, *Group* and *Virtue*."